OUR DESPERATE BRIDE

LACEY DAVIS

VIRTUAL BOOKSELLER LLC

Even promises of a new beginning come with a price.

Daisy Miller was the belle of the ball until she was involved in scandal. Even her parents have disowned her and she has been reduced to living on the streets of Charleston. Then she overhears a professional matchmaker looking for mail-order brides. Could this be her chance to start over? Could there be a place she could overcome her shame?

Ellis Sanders and Lee Chapman are successful businessmen, but each of their past mistakes have the potential to destroy their futures. Though not actively searching for a bride, they're both smitten with the elusive Daisy.

Can a woman heal their wounds or will she only ignite their demons and bring the errs of their ways alive?

CHAPTER 1

*D*esperately searching for a place to hide, Daisy Miller ran through the streets of Charleston. For the last week, her life had been a living hell. She darted into an alley then ducked behind trash cans. The smell of rotting food almost made her gag.

Going from ball gowns, to living on the streets, what else could happen to her?

"Oh, Daisy, I'm going to find you," the man said with a laugh. "Soon, a fine upstanding young woman like yourself, once a debutante, will be working in the whorehouse. Business will be great as all the men in town come to spread your legs. Sample what Thomas got a taste of."

A tremble of fear had her body shaking as she tried not to breathe, hoping he would tire of hunting for her and go on. Tears filled her eyes and part of her wanted to give up.

Since the night of the scandal, her life had gone from parties to searching for help with nowhere to go. Not believing her claim she was almost raped, her father and

1

mother had sided with Thomas Jones and his lie that he took her virginity. They had forbidden her from staying at their home, so she would not influence her sisters. Also, hoping to force Thomas to marry her.

But he didn't care.

What kind of father would kick his daughter out of the house with nowhere to go? What kind of father would take the side of the man instead of his daughters? A father who so desperately wanted the man's business in his work.

None of this was her fault, and yet, she suffered the consequences of that evil man's actions. Somehow she would destroy him, but right now, she was just doing her best to survive on the streets, scrounging for food and shelter. Doing her best to hide from men like this who wanted to trap her and make her into a whore.

She would die first.

She peeked around the trash cans, knowing she couldn't stay there all night. The alley wall she leaned against belonged to a bar, and soon, they would come out to dump their garbage. She would be found. Glancing down at the once beautiful dress she had worn that night, she wanted to cry, but crying would not get her anything to eat.

And she was starving.

The first night, she had crawled beneath an old blanket she found and cried herself to sleep in the park, but it was a dangerous place. A place where others like herself roamed at night.

How could her father and mother abandon her like this? She had never done anything wrong and suddenly they said she was scandalous. They thought she was lying when the most eligible man in Charleston tried to force her to have sex with him.

Standing, she tried to brush the dirt from her gown. Time to move on before the police found her and arrested her for vagrancy. She'd been threatened once, but where could she go?

Stepping out of the alley, she glanced down the street where she had walked with her mother, her head held high, laughing with her sisters, and shopping. No more.

They had disowned her.

With a glance, she noticed a woman putting up a flyer on a tree that led into the park. The park where she had spent the last few nights hiding behind the bushes, wrapped in a dirty blanket, struggling to stay hidden.

The woman glanced at her, and Daisy knew she looked bad.

"What are you posting?"

The woman glanced at her, her eyes widened but she didn't look down on her. Instead there was sympathy in her gaze.

"I need women who want to become mail-order brides," she said. "Eight women to go to Treasure Falls, Montana, where they will have a husband waiting to take care of them. These men will even pay your way back if you don't like them or Treasure Falls."

No one would know her in Montana. She would have a husband who would care for her. Give her the family she'd lost. No one would know of her shame or the deceit she'd experienced.

"When are they leaving?"

"Not until I find eight women. Right now, I only have one. But if you need a place to stay until the train leaves, I have room."

No more sleeping on the ground, worried someone would find her. Or someone trying to…

No more running from the man who owned the whorehouse.

"What about food? I'm starving," she confessed to the woman.

"You're Daisy Miller, aren't you," the woman said.

"Yes, but I was—almost raped," she said, her voice dropping low. "I didn't want him to touch me."

"You're still a virgin?"

"Yes," she said as a tear slipped down her face. No one believed her. They all believed that horrible man Thomas. And he was spreading vicious lies about her that her father thought were true.

"Let me help you," the woman said in a kind tone. "It would be a new start for you, and you could escape the scandal."

Oh, how she wanted her family to take her in. To believe in her. Oh, how she wanted her sisters to welcome her back with open arms, but she didn't think they would. They all believed the horrible stories being spread about her.

If she stayed here, what were her chances of finding a good husband? Of finding a man who didn't believe the lies?

Not good.

With a sigh, she knew her chance for a good life was impossible here. Even if she proved her innocence, she was ruined. This could be a new start, a new beginning.

A sense of peace filled her and she knew this was what she needed.

"All right, but I can't stay on the streets any longer. That horrible man who owns the whorehouse is trying to find me. He wants to turn me into a whore."

The woman glanced around uneasily. "Come with me. You can stay at my place. We'll get you a meal, a bath, and even some pretty new clothes to wear."

Tears filled Daisy's eyes. "You believe that I did nothing wrong?"

The woman took her by the arm. "Honey, for thousands of years, women have been subjected to men trying to rape them and then blaming the women when caught. You're not the first, and you won't be the last. But you can start your life over in a beautiful new location. You're young. You're beautiful, and the men in Montana are going to fight over you. Let's get you home."

For the first time in days, Daisy felt hope. She felt relief and security—things she'd taken for granted before. But never again. Never again would she trust a man. Never again would she be the subject of scandal.

She'd kill the next man who tried to take advantage of her. She'd do her best to get even with Thomas Jones even from as far away as Montana.

CHAPTER 2

*D*aisy read the Charleston newspaper society pages and wanted to throw up. Already Thomas Jones had moved on to his next victim. A young girl barely sixteen.

As grateful as she was to Mrs. Newton for saving her from the streets, she had to do something. Tomorrow they were leaving town, and while she knew she could never stop Thomas, she could not leave without getting her revenge.

Somehow she had to tell the world that he was not a good man.

But how?

No one would listen to her. No one believed that he had forced himself on her…that only by the grace of God had he not completely defiled her and taken her virginity.

Everyone believed he was a fine, upstanding young man who was the catch of the season. Everyone but her.

What could she do?

Getting up and walking downstairs, she suddenly had an idea. Could it work? No, it wasn't earth shattering, but it would let the women of Charleston be aware that the man was a predator of young women.

What if there were other victims who hid in shame?

She ran outside to Mrs. Newton's barn. Inside were wood, nails, paint, and everything she needed. After she closed the barn door, she took off her beautiful dress, and in her pantaloons and chemise, she painted a piece of wood she found. After she wrote in red paint the words, she found some wiring and made a hanger.

Staring at her handiwork, she put her dress back on. Maybe it wouldn't help, maybe no one would see her creation, but she had to do something. She had to try to save the young woman he was pursuing and any other women in town he might try to defile.

After she put her dress on, she went upstairs and wrote the girl's father a note. Borrowing money from Mary, she paid a courier to take it to him in the morning. Then she found Blanche Underwood, another young woman leaving with her tomorrow for Treasure Falls.

Blanche was nicknamed the "wild one" because she could outshoot, outride, and do anything a man could, and did not know how to be a lady. Mrs. Newton had been working with her, but frankly, the girl couldn't care less about holding tea parties. She wanted to ride horses bareback across the fields.

"Blanche, I need your help," Daisy whispered.

The girl looked up, her auburn tresses hung down her

back and her emerald eyes gazed at her quizzically. "What do you need?"

"Not here," Daisy said, glancing at the other young women who sat around crocheting or doing needlework. They all looked like such perfect young ladies, but most of them had a past.

"Meet me out by the barn," Daisy told her.

Mary frowned across the room at them. She knew that something was up, but she said very little and never left the house. Not once in the two weeks that Daisy had been here, had she seen her outside. This was the first time she'd seen her down in the parlor.

Daisy sat and waited for Blanche to slip out the door, and a few minutes later, she joined her outside. The women had not even noticed when she disappeared. Most of them were quiet. They all knew that in the morning they were leaving. That's why this was the perfect time for Daisy to do this.

She opened the barn door. "You know what happened to me, right?"

"Yes," Blanche said. "My papa said I would never be a debutante because of men like him. Too many scalawags."

"He was right," Daisy told her. "I need your help. Tonight, late, I want to sneak out and hang this sign on the Jones's house, on his gate so everyone will see it in the morning."

Blanche laughed. "Oh, this sounds like what I've been missing. I've felt so stifled sitting around in that house all day just waiting for the time for us to leave. I'm sick of it.

Needlepoint bores me and the women are so depressing. Wish I didn't have to leave."

Daisy could not disagree with the woman, but she didn't have the owner of the whorehouse trying to catch her and put her to work. In the weeks since Daisy had been kicked out of the house, her family had not tried to find her as far as she knew. She really had no choice but to leave.

"Agreed. What do you think of my sign?"

The girl smiled and read. "Beware Defiler Rapist. Guard Your Daughters."

Getting the words on there had been difficult, but somehow she'd managed. Two simple lines of text told the people of Charleston who lived in the big mansion on the hill.

"I'm so excited. We'll need to slip out around midnight, sneak through the streets, and then put this on his gate."

Daisy didn't tell her about the note she'd sent to the young woman's father. That, no one needed to know about but herself.

"I'll meet you out here at midnight," Blanche told her. "I'm so excited we're doing this."

A thrill scurried down Daisy's spine. Yes, she was taking a chance, but she was also getting even. And, hopefully, her note to the sixteen-year-old's papa would end Thomas's chances with her.

Five hours later as the clock struck midnight, she put on her pinned-together ball dress that the hornswoggle had ripped. She rushed out of the house and met Blanche at the barn. The girl was wearing dark men's clothing.

9

"You look great," Daisy told her. "If I'd some men's clothing I would have done the same."

"Sorry, I only saved the one set. I'm hoping once I get settled, I can wear them again."

The girl was stunningly beautiful and all that auburn hair of hers was pulled back and piled up under a hat. No, she didn't look like a man. She looked like a beautiful woman disguised as a man. There was no hiding her voluptuous curves. Curves even Daisy felt a little jealous of.

"Let's get this done and get back. We're leaving in a few hours," Daisy said, glad to finally be getting on the train out of town. She'd never been out of Charleston, and the thought of leaving her family behind made her sad, but she needed to leave if she wanted a new life.

She had to get out of Charleston.

"Let's go," Blanche said, picking up the sign. "Grab some more wire. Let's make this difficult for him to remove."

"I like your way of thinking," Daisy told her, grabbing the small spool of bendable wire.

They opened the barn door, glanced out, and then took the back alleys to the mansion that sat upon a small rise in the middle of town. They were quiet, and when they heard voices, they hid in the shrubbery until two drunks went stumbling down the street.

"Geez, it's past midnight. Don't they know they should be home?" Daisy whispered, remembering her nights sleeping in the park, hidden in bushes with mosquitoes and ants biting her. It had been a horrible time that she never wanted to repeat in her life, and yet, here she was taking a chance.

But she had to. She had to get her revenge before she left town.

They reached the gate and stood there for a moment watching to make certain Thomas didn't have guards or someone watching the house. No one. It was silent.

Quickly they worked on hanging the crudely made sign on the gate, wrapping wire around the iron rods so it would take a while to disassemble.

When they finished, they stood back and admired their handiwork. Giggling quietly, they ran down the street toward the alleys that led them back to Mrs. Newton's home.

It was finished. No matter what happened tomorrow, she had done her best to alert the women of Charleston that the man would harm them just like he'd harmed her.

When they reached the house, they snuck back inside. Daisy hugged Blanche.

"Thank you. That meant a lot to me."

"You're welcome. That was the most fun I've had in two weeks. Now, we better get to bed. We have a long day tomorrow."

The girls went to their separate bedrooms and Daisy undressed and crawled under the sheets. She tossed the old ball gown, leaving it behind.

Tomorrow her new life began, but tonight she had written hopefully the final chapter in her dealings with Mr. Thomas Jones. Hopefully, he would now be the one who would face society's condemnation.

CHAPTER 3

*A*ll morning, Daisy felt as nervous as a newborn filly. Any moment, she feared the sheriff would be pounding on the door to arrest her. Finally, they were at the train station and she couldn't wait to start the journey to her new life.

With a sigh, she stepped out of the carriage that had taken her and the other ladies to the train station. She glanced around at the people boarding and knew these were her final moments in Charleston, the city of her birth. The place her family resided. The family that had disowned her and kicked her out of the house with no means of support. The family she still loved with all her heart.

"Does everyone have their tickets," Mrs. Newton asked the ladies.

Daisy held up hers.

"Now, girls, remember, you can come back to

Charleston if this is not what you want. They will pay your way home."

Doubtfully, that would happen. She could be betrothed to an ogre and she would not return home to Charleston, ever.

Just then she saw the police walking down the platform. Oh no, no.

He stopped in front of Mrs. Newton, and she pointed to Daisy, and then she walked beside them.

Her heart was pounding in her chest, but she held her head high and refused to be intimidated by them.

"Daisy, these men want to talk to you."

"Make it quick, I'm about to get on this train and start my life over."

"Did you hang a sign on Mr. Jones's house last night?"

Daisy jerked back and stared at the lawman. "I was busy packing and preparing for my trip this morning. I didn't have time for that scalawag Thomas Jones. What kind of sign are you talking about?"

The man studied her. "He's the man who ruined you?"

"Yes, but what does that have to do with a sign?"

With a sigh, he gazed at her, staring into her eyes and she returned his stare, not willing to back down. She was not going to jail.

"Someone hung a sign on his gate that said *beware defiler rapist.*"

She started laughing. "Good for them. If you find out who did it, please tell them I said thank you."

The man recoiled.

"Now, if you'll excuse me, I'm going to Treasure Falls, Montana, as a mail-order bride. My new life awaits me away from men like Mr. Jones who society thinks is a good man."

The officer held out his arm and laid it on hers. "And you're certain of your innocence?"

She laughed. "Completely. I have been innocent all this time. Now I'm going to a place where society will not judge a woman so unfairly."

With a sigh, he stepped back and shook his head at her. "Against my better judgment, I'm going to let you go. Good luck, Miss Miller."

"Thank you," she said and then turned to Mrs. Newton. "Thank you for helping me. I fear where I would have wound up if not for you."

"You're welcome, dear, now get on that train. Your new life awaits you."

Daisy picked up her carpetbag that held the few things she'd managed to obtain. She walked across the wooden deck and stepped onto the train.

The conductor took her ticket and showed her to her seat. When she passed by Blanche, she winked at her.

And the two women giggled, sharing a secret.

She sank down across from Mary and glanced out the windows of the train. Her chest filled with unshed tears and she tried not to let them reach her eyes. She was on her way to a new beginning. A new life.

But there were so many things that she loved that she was leaving behind. Including her sisters. Her parents…

well, her heart had hardened against them when they threw her out of the house, but still she loved them.

"To new beginnings," she said under her breath.

"To new beginnings," Mary replied.

The train whistle blew and the engine began to chug toward her destiny.

CHAPTER 4

*L*ee Chapman and his good friend Ellis Sanders, part of the Sanders family who were the wealthiest in town and owned most of the businesses in Treasure Falls, both had lucrative establishments. After the war, Ellis went home to Montana to run the family bank while Lee followed to operate the local mercantile.

It was a legitimate business, and it made enough money that Lee could afford what he wanted. Before his mother died, he would send home money for her and his sister. But now Mother was gone.

Beth he worried about daily. For the last six months, he'd been helping her, and he wanted her to move to Treasure Falls from Helena, Montana, but she refused.

Once a month, he sent her a hundred dollars hoping that would keep her out of trouble.

He glanced through her latest letter and feared for her safety. Seems that after his mother died, the landlord decided he didn't want a single woman occupying the house she was renting.

The old buzzard had been trying to get them out of it for years. Now, Lee regretted not buying the dang place from the old man. But he always hoped Beth would move out here, and so far, she was staying put.

"Is she doing all right?" Ellis asked as they walked toward their home.

The sun was setting over the mountains, casting a pink glow off the snow-capped tops. He'd never lived in a prettier place, and he would never leave Treasure Falls. The pine trees, the rivers, the fields of flowers in the spring felt like home.

And he genuinely liked the people in their small mountain town.

He lifted his cowboy hat and pushed his dark sandy hair back. "I worry about her. It's not safe for a woman to be living alone, especially in Helena."

"She'd have her pick of husbands if she came to Treasure Falls," Ellis said.

Ellis's family, specifically his uncle and aunt, had started the town, though the hardships had been plenty to begin. The winters were cold, food could become scarce, and the blizzards were dangerous.

But there wasn't a more beautiful spot in Montana.

"I've asked her repeatedly. There's a man she says that she loves and she's waiting for him to ask her to marry him."

Ellis frowned. "How long has she been waiting?"

"Almost a year," Lee said, frowning. "I've told her it's

time to forget about James. If he hasn't asked her by now, it's past time. I wish to God she would listen."

Ellis glanced at him and frowned. "If the landlord kicked her out, where is she living?"

That had troubled him most of all, and he also wondered what happened to the personal belongings in the house.

"A room in a boarding house," he said, knowing that sometimes those places could become dens of ill repute. Beth had no one in town besides her friends. Why would she not listen to reason and move here to Treasure Falls with him?

"Do you want to ride over to Helena and check on her?"

It was a tempting thought, but any day now, the women should be arriving. Any day now, they could be meeting their future wife and he was not about to miss that glorious day. He'd waited plenty long enough.

"No, I'm not going anywhere until after the brides arrive," he said.

Ellis nodded. The man didn't seem near as keen on getting married as Lee was. In fact, Ellis had only reluctantly agreed to the idea because Lee wanted a wife and family so badly.

The only requirement from Lee was that there were two husbands, not one. A woman alone didn't have a chance in this world of raising children and putting food on the table. He'd witnessed it firsthand, and he would never leave his woman and children starving if something happened to him.

"Are you ready to get married?" Lee asked Ellis.

His friend, who was more like a brother, glanced at him. "I'll do what I need to do. Just don't expect me to fall in love with her and be a great husband. But I must say I can't wait to fuck her."

Lee grinned at him. "Thinking with your dick again."

"Hell, I think with my dick way more than I should. It's what keeps me in trouble."

Lee knew what he was talking about, but he refused to bring up the subject. Not many people in town knew about his tragic love affair that had deeply scarred him.

"Are you certain this is what you want to do?" Lee asked, knowing that Ellis agreed to this marriage because of Lee's desire for a family. He missed his mother and sister. He missed being part of a group of people who looked out for one another.

"Yes," he said. "Don't worry about me. As long as the fucking is good, I'm in. Besides, my family is clamoring for the town to grow and get bigger. We're supposed to have lots of babies who grow up to make this town prosper."

His family, the Sanders, pretty much ran the town and were justified for paying for women to come here as mail-order brides. Ellis's older brother who owned the local mine had paid for eight women to come to Treasure Falls. Eight hopefully gorgeous, young, marriage-minded women who wanted to settle down and start a family. Exactly what Lee was wanting.

He was relieved. There wasn't a woman here in town that interested him. No one that he fantasized about wanting to put his dick inside her cunny. No woman here in town that made him dream about raising her skirts and sinking deep inside her, paddling her ass, and making her theirs.

For the last three months, he'd been wondering what the women would look like. Would they find someone they both agreed upon for their wife? How long would they have to wait before they married her and took her home to claim her as their own?

"Don't you think they found the women awfully quick? I mean, I would think it would take a while for them to find eight women who would agree to have two husbands."

Ellis was right. From the last letter received from the matchmaker, the women were on their way and should be here in the middle to the end of June, depending on the weather.

"Agree, but maybe things are still really bad back east. The war has been over for ten years, but still we were stupid young'uns when we agreed to fight. Thank God, we made it out alive and came to our senses."

They had met at the battle of Jonesborough, Georgia, and had marched into the city of Atlanta together. That was in the fall of 1864 and they had been best friends ever since. In fact, when they were released from the army, they spent three days at a bordello in Kansas City before catching a boat and coming home to Montana.

Those had been the worst days of his life, and now at the ripe old age of thirty, he knew it was time to have his own family. Children and a wife to replace the ones he'd lost.

"You won't catch me signing up to go to war for anyone again," Ellis said softly.

"Agreed," said Lee. "But I have to say, we've done well since we returned home to Montana."

"Yes, we have," Ellis said.

Even though when they returned, they had learned that Ellis's parents had died in a mine explosion. Many miners were either hurt or killed that day. And Ellis sought comfort in Arianna's arms.

"Let's hope that with our bride arriving in the next couple of weeks, our good fortune continues."

"I just want to fuck her," Ellis said with a laugh. "It's been a long time since my cock was surrounded by a warm, wet pussy."

Lee shook his head. "That kind of attitude is not going to impress a lady. We need to make certain that we treat her well."

Ellis sighed. "You're right, but again, I'm thinking with my cock. Look, I know I'm not near as excited as you are, but I'll do my best to make her happy and to treat her well."

It was true. He had no doubts that Ellis would eventually come around, but the man had suffered a terrible heartache that ended in tragedy, and love didn't come easy for him. In fact, for over two years, he had avoided women.

"Let's get home," Lee said. "We need to clean our house and get it ready for a woman."

"Yes," Ellis said. "Things will definitely change when we bring in a wife."

CHAPTER 5

*D*aisy knew she was completely out of her element. For two nights, the women on the stage had slept along the trail with the drivers keeping watch. Each night, the sound of the coyotes had sung them to sleep.

She'd been terrified, certain the creatures were going to snack on them as soon as they closed their eyes.

This was definitely not Charleston. The air was cooler and the mountains in the distance still had snow on their rugged tops. Sometimes fear would overwhelm her from the risk she'd taken and then she would remember the nights sleeping in the park and the man from the bordello searching for her.

Oh no, this life would be different, but she would adjust. She had no choice.

The trip by train had been the best and the boat had not been bad, but the stage was like riding a bucking horse in a box and she had the bruises to prove it. And yet not a one of the women complained.

There were a couple of women she wasn't certain were going to make it, but when things got rough, everyone seemed to do their best to help each other. She had learned to do laundry whenever she got a chance and a fresh bath was heaven.

One night, Blanche had been ill and Daisy had made her a cup of tea and sat up with her. It must have been a touch of food poisoning because soon she was over it.

They were all in this together, and though she was certain all of them knew her past, she also wondered what secrets they were hiding. What had forced them to leave Charleston?

Daisy couldn't imagine not being happy in Treasure Falls and making a return trip to Charleston. The three months had been long and oftentimes dangerous. She was not returning unless she learned her husband was a cannibal and even then she'd tell him he didn't want to eat her tough flesh.

Today was the last day of the journey. At the last stop, the driver told them they would be there within the hour and the women had grown quiet and tense.

It was the beginning of their new lives.

A man. A wedding. A husband. And soon a family. She thought of her sisters and wondered if they and her mother had searched for her in town. Did anyone miss her?

The horses seemed to pick up speed like they knew

they were in the home stretch. The tension inside the coach was almost tangible.

Suddenly they were rolling into town and she gasped.

It was small. Smaller than she ever imagined. She'd pictured a city like Charleston, but this town was only a couple of blocks long. There was a bank, a mercantile, a restaurant, and a saloon.

Houses sat back from the main area of town and the largest house had a sign out front—Dr. Owen Sanders.

Daisy glanced at Mary, suddenly fearful they would soon find themselves in a bordello. "No hotel? Where will we stay?"

For the last couple of miles, they had held each other's hand. Shaking at what they would soon face. Today, they would learn if they had chosen wisely or made a huge mistake coming to Treasure Falls.

"I don't know. Look, there is a group of people standing in front of a building. Oh, dear, it's the men."

Daisy began to shake even harder. The two women turned and grabbed each other, sharing a hug. They had become great friends. In fact, there wasn't a woman on the two stages that Daisy didn't like. Sure, they were women, sometimes catty, but they were sharing an experience of a lifetime.

One they would tell their children about someday.

"We'll always be friends," Daisy said, tears filling her eyes.

"Yes, always. No matter what happens," Mary said.

Rose and Blanche, the other two women who shared

their stage, were all but hanging out the windows, trying to catch a glimpse of the men. Their future husbands.

The stagecoach driver pulled on the reins, and the horses slowed, bringing the coach to a stop.

"This is it," Mary said.

Daisy couldn't speak. There was a loud roar from the men gathered to greet them.

"Oh, look how handsome they all are," Blanche said. "We're getting married."

The door suddenly opened. "Ladies, you have arrived."

Dear God, this was it. At the last stop, they had thrown dice to see who would alight first and in what order. Mary had won the draw and Daisy was second. Frankly, she wanted to be last, but she knew there was no holding back.

Her heart was jumping inside her chest, pounding with anxiety and fear. What if her husband was just like Thomas?

No, she refused to believe that she could travel all this way and find another scalawag.

Swallowing, she watched as Mary took the driver's hand and stepped from the stage. Then it was Daisy's turn.

She glanced at the other women. "Good luck."

"You too," they said.

When she stepped from the stage, the sun warmed her cheeks and she took a deep breath to calm her nerves. The air smelled so clean and fresh, and suddenly her nerves calmed.

Following Mary, she was greeted by a man named Jesse. Then an older woman grabbed her hand.

"Welcome, I'm Grace Sanders. You'll be staying in our

home until you marry," she said, smiling. "We're so excited to have you ladies. Welcome to Treasure Falls."

Daisy felt a nervous giggle bubbling up from her. People here were just as nice as back home. "Thank you. I am Daisy Miller."

A dark-haired man stepped in front of her and she glanced up into the most beautiful blue eyes and shadowy lashes. He gripped her hand. "Lee Chapman, welcome to Treasure Falls. We're so excited that you're here."

The man winked at her. For some reason, she felt herself warm. She'd been so afraid that after what happened in Charleston, she'd be afraid of men. But this man seemed to put her at ease.

He had a beautiful smile that warmed her clear to her toes. Funny, but she'd never reacted to a man like this before.

"Thank you. Daisy Miller," she said almost breathless. A tingle of awareness spiraled through her straight to her center.

"I own and run the mercantile here in town," he said.

"That's a very important business in a town like this."

"Yes, ma'am, it is," he said.

Another more somber man stepped up beside Lee. Glancing at him, she couldn't help but wonder at the size of these men. Was it the mountain air or the water they drank? Big arms with muscular chests and hands that could grip and hold a woman tight.

But not too tight.

"Ellis Sanders," he said. "Welcome to Treasure Falls. I run the local bank."

The man did not look like any banker she'd ever met. These men put the society gentlemen in Charleston to shame. They were more like lumberjacks, and she had the strangest urge to reach out and touch their big forearms. Feel all that muscular strength.

She smiled. "Daisy Miller. I must say you look more like a rancher than a banker."

He grinned. "Thank you. My family owns a ranching business. I take care of all our banking needs here in town."

Blanche was behind her and gave her a little nudge. But she really didn't want to leave these two men. If she had her way, she'd tell Blanche to just move around her.

"We'll see you later this evening," Lee said. "Don't sit with anyone but us."

She grinned. "All right."

Warmth filled her at the thought that they had already laid claim to her from the other men and she was glad. A banker and a mercantile owner. Not too bad.

She moved on down the line of men, meeting each one. But there was something about Lee and Ellis that drew her. She couldn't help but think about their big hands skimming down her arm, their full lips kissing her. But she would have to choose which one she wanted. She couldn't be greedy.

For a moment, she was shocked. After everything that Thomas had done, she had been so afraid that she could not get over his near rape. But these two men were strong and yet gentle. Or so they seemed.

When she reached the end of the line, she stood next to Mary.

When everyone was off the stage, Jesse Sanders whistled loud enough to get everyone's attention.

"We're having a supper tonight at Uncle Owen and Aunt Grace's home at six thirty. For now, we're going to let the ladies get settled in, clean the dust off, and rest before the evening's festivities."

His aunt smiled at everyone. "We have a pig roasting and our cook is making lots of good food for tonight. You are to dress in clean attire to meet these ladies. And, of course, we will expect everyone to be on their very best behavior."

Aunt Grace walked to the front of the line. "Follow me, ladies."

Daisy couldn't help but turn and glance back at Lee and Ellis. Lee grinned at her and winked again. Ellis seemed to be gazing at the back of her dress.

Of all the men she'd met, Lee was the one she felt drawn to the most. But Ellis was a close second. But how would she decide between the two of them? Not one but two handsome men wanting to court her.

CHAPTER 6

*E*llis couldn't help but watch as Daisy walked down Main Street toward his aunt and uncle's house. He had not planned on becoming infatuated or even interested in any of the women. Sure, he knew he would have to marry one of them, but he was going to let Lee find the woman he wanted, and then he would go along with his choice.

Once you've been in love and had your heart broken, you're more cautious and couldn't care less about love a second time around.

But when the blonde stepped off the stage, his cock had gone hard, his palms became sweaty, his heart pounded in his chest and it was all he could do not to scoop her up and carry her to their house. Daisy had long lashes that swept down over her sky-blue eyes, sweet cherry lips, a cute little nose that turned up at the end, and a smile that had him dreaming of her mouth around his cock.

Her long blonde hair was curled down her back and he

imagined his hands threaded through those curls, pulling her soft mouth to his.

Now, the two men just stood there in the street, watching her walk to the house, mesmerized by the sway of her full hips.

"Good God," Lee said, his voice had that breathless sound when he was about to come. "That woman is a piece of art. Why in the world is she not married?"

"Good question," Ellis said, thinking there must be something wrong with her. Some reason that the men in Charleston had not snatched her up and carried her to the church. Some reason that right now his cock wouldn't even listen to.

"Did you see those curves? Full breasts, tiny waist, and hips that a man can grab onto while he's shoving his cock in her."

"Down boy," Ellis said with a laugh, knowing that he was having the same reaction. But he would never admit that to Lee.

"Did you see any other woman that made your cock stand at attention? When Daisy stepped off that stage, it was like my heart leaped into my throat and my cock did a dance in my pants."

Ellis shook his head at his friend. Now that they both had successful businesses here in town the only thing they needed was a wife. But Ellis was not as crazy about the idea until now. Today had changed everything.

"Really? Your cock was dancing in your pants?" Ellis said, laughing at his friend. They had shared many women while they were traveling, but he'd never mentioned his cock could dance. That was a sight that Ellis wasn't certain he wanted to see.

"It would have been doing more, but I told him to settle down. That hopefully that pussy would soon be ours."

Of the two of them, Lee was more outgoing and could have a room laughing in no time. But Ellis knew that underneath the laughter, there was heartache. The man longed for a family to replace the mother and father he'd lost. Though his sister lived in Helena, he seldom saw her, unless she needed money.

Lee wanted a family. A wife. Children.

Ellis was more cautious than his friend. He'd already screwed up his chance at getting a family once, and he was afraid of how it would go down the second time around. But this woman definitely caught his interest.

Walking toward the home they shared, they passed the bank and the mercantile, which were right next to each other. Both businesses were closed at the moment, but come Monday morning, they would be open bright and early.

Along the wooden sidewalk, their boots clunked. A necessity in the wintertime when the road was covered in snow. And in the spring when a river of mud filled the street.

"Just think in a couple of weeks, we could be bringing Miss Daisy home," Lee said excited.

Already, Lee had made up his mind. Ellis glanced down the street where he'd lived since he was a boy. His aunt and uncle and his parents started Treasure Falls and now his family was trying to continue the growth of the little town.

After seeing the destruction of the South during the war, he'd longed to come home and plant solid roots right here where he grew up.

"Maybe, if we agree she's the one," Ellis said being more cautious.

A breeze blew and the sun beat down on them. Ellis was glad that the nights were cooler than the day. Tonight he wanted to get to know Daisy better. See if she was who they were looking for. Find out why no one in Charleston wanted her. Why she'd left everything she knew behind and traveled so far.

While he would let Lee do the choosing, he had to keep a tight rein on his heart. Having it broken once was tough, but a second time would be devastating.

Old Man Cox stepped out of the shadows right into their path. This was not what he needed today. Especially today.

"You son of a bitch," he screamed and ran toward Ellis.

The man was drunk and Ellis wasn't afraid of him. At five feet ten inches and weighing maybe a hundred seventy-five, life had not been good to Henry Cox. And he blamed all his problems on Ellis.

"Henry, don't do this," Lee said, stepping between him and Ellis. "You're drunk."

"Of course, I am," the old man said, spitting in the dirt in front of Ellis. "I should kill you."

"Right now, your aim is a little unsteady," Lee said.

The man snarled at him almost like a rabid dog.

Maybe he should, Ellis couldn't help but think. At least then, the both of them wouldn't be hurting any longer.

"Go ahead, if that's what you want to do," Ellis said. He was tired of fighting him. He was tired of the guilt the man riddled him with. The pain he lived with daily. He'd rather take a bullet and then it would be over.

The old man stumbled. "Hell, no, you need to suffer."

"Should I get the sheriff," Lee asked.

"Go ahead. I don't care," Henry said. "I've spent many a night in jail."

Lately, it seemed like he spent every other week behind bars. Ellis had stopped contacting the sheriff. What was the point? The old man had threatened but never carried out those threats.

"You killed my babies," he said with a slur. "You took away the people I loved."

There was no point in arguing with the man. But it was all Ellis could do to keep from screaming back at him. It didn't have to end the way it had. Ellis felt horrible about their deaths, but it had been out of his control.

Henry was as much to blame for Arianna's death as anyone.

Shaking, the man glared at him. "If you think you're going to marry one of these girls and be happy, you've got another thing coming. I'll do everything I can to make certain you're miserable. After I'm done, you'll be living in pain."

Like he wasn't already.

Lee stepped in front of the old man. Ellis could see that the man had crossed the line with that comment.

"Henry, don't even think about interfering with our

marriage. Do you understand me? It will be the last thing you ever do. I'll make certain of it."

The man jerked back and Ellis could see that he was surprised that Lee wasn't just standing by like normal.

"Now, I would recommend that you go home and sleep it off. Because tonight is a special night for us and I don't want your nonsense ruining it, do you understand?"

The old man glanced between the two of them, his lip curled up in a disgusting grimace. "You'll never be happy. I'll make certain of it."

"Get out of here before I kick your drunk ass," Lee said.

For the first time since Henry had taken to harassing Ellis, Lee expressed his frustration. Threatening their new wife would get Henry six feet under if he wasn't careful.

Turning, the old man almost fell over as he stumbled, heading toward home. As he careened down the street, he pulled out a whiskey bottle and took a big drink.

"Never seen you so upset," Ellis said, wishing that Henry would not do this. It only made things worse.

"Look, I get it. Life dealt him some bad blows. Some we know he brought on himself. But he better not interfere with our woman, our family, or try to destroy us, because I will not put up with his nonsense."

With a sigh, Ellis slapped him on the back. "Let me see if I can get him some help."

"No," Lee said. "That's the problem. He hates you, and you've done everything you can to be good to him. It's time to kick his ass, and if you're not willing, I am."

But that was the problem. Ellis felt guilty and he couldn't kick the old man's ass. No matter what, he understood his pain and felt some of it himself. But he'd never seen Lee come unhinged like this before regarding Henry.

"Come on, let's get home. We've got to get all cleaned up, so we can go and court our wife."

A smile crossed Lee's face and they turned to home once again. With a sigh, Lee glanced at him and smiled.

"How are we going to persuade her that we're the ones she's been looking for?"

Ellis laughed. "Flirting is your department. I'm just there to show her what she's going to be missing if she doesn't choose us."

Lee smiled. "I'm going to kiss her tonight."

"No, I get the first kiss," Ellis said, knowing his teasing would help diffuse the situation with Henry.

"Like hell."

"We'll draw for it," Ellis said.

"All right, let's do this. Whoever kisses her first, the other one, when we marry, gets her virginity."

Ellis sighed. "Well, hell, now you've ruined it for me. You can have the damn kiss. I'll claim her first."

Lee shook his head. "Changed my mind. You can kiss her first."

They walked up to their two-story house. Lee glanced up at the windows. "Just think, we could soon be fucking her in that big bed upstairs. And nine months later we could have a son or a daughter."

It was a wonderful idea, but Ellis had already lost one child. He could not go through losing another.

"Let's start with tonight."

CHAPTER 7

*T*he closer the time came for the party, the more nervous Daisy became. She and Mary were sharing a room at the Owens's house.

"What if I can't do this, Mary?" she asked. "Since the attempted rape, no man has kissed me or looked at me. What if I start screaming when they touch me?"

Mary walked over to her and took her hands. "Daisy, let it go. I know that what Thomas did to you was wrong, but this is a different city. A different life and these men are different."

That was true, but the memory of Thomas tying her wrists together then pulling down her bodice exposing her breasts and the struggle she put up fighting him until he slapped her, caused panic to race through her. And yet her father had believed him when Thomas said that she was willing, even encouraging him to take her.

With a sigh, she did her best to erase the memory of that night.

"What should I tell them when they ask me why I left Charleston? I don't want to tell that sordid story and have them gaze at me with pity, or even worse, no longer believing I'm a virgin," she said, hanging her head.

Why did such a horrible event happen to her?

But she wouldn't be here in Treasure Falls if the attempted rape had not happened. Now, it was time to turn that horrible time into something that made her happy.

"Look at me," Mary said. "You're beautiful. You tell them there were no men in Charleston you were interested in. It's not a total lie, and after what Thomas did, no man would have you, so it works."

With a sigh, she knew Mary was right, but what if they tried to kiss her? How would she react?

"Thank you, Mary. You always make me feel better."

It was true, she had become such a good friend.

"Are you ready?"

"Yes," Daisy said.

"Now remember, smile, laugh, and have fun. You deserve to be happy. You deserve this second chance," Mary told her.

Daisy stared at her friend. She knew she had a secret, but Mary had never told her. One day, she hoped Mary would trust her enough to confide in her what happened to send her running, because she had been on the run.

With a deep breath, she smiled. "I will. Now, what man are you looking at?"

"Andrew Larsen, though his friend Jesse Sanders is not bad either."

They had been the first men to greet them when they

stepped off the stage, but Daisy still had her eyes on Lee and his friend Ellis.

"How about you?"

"Oh, Lee is the one that I immediately felt drawn to."

"Well, let's go meet our new husbands," Mary said as Aunt Grace knocked on the door. As she opened the door, a smile spread across her face. "See you downstairs."

Daisy tried to calm her rapidly beating heart as Aunt Grace motioned it was her time to walk downstairs.

She lifted the front of her yellow gown and stepped outside onto the landing and then strolled down the stairs, her head held high, a smile on her face as she gazed at the eager eyes watching her descend.

No longer would she let what Thomas did to her affect her in any way. Tonight she was going to take charge of her life and start over. This was the new beginning she deserved.

When she reached the floor, the doctor came over and escorted her to stand by Mary. Then the other girls came down the stairs until they all were in the same room.

The doctor stood between the men and women.

"Welcome, ladies, we're so glad you're here. Tonight is a chance for all of you to get to know one another. The men will tell you who their partner is so you'll get to know both of the men at once. You have two weeks to make up your mind before we will have a wedding ceremony right here in the house. You'll marry one man and the other will be your second husband."

What? Did he just say they would have two husbands?

She glanced at Mary who was standing there stiff and Daisy could see she was just as stunned as she was.

"Excuse me," Rose Patton said. "What are you talking about two husbands?"

There was chattering among the women.

"In Treasure Falls, there are two husbands for each woman. We have lived this way for many years due to the shortage of women. This way if one husband is killed, the second man is there to make certain the family is taken care of."

Shocked, Daisy didn't know what to think. And yet, she could not return to Charleston. Not only would she have nowhere to go, but Thomas would most definitely be trying to find her and punish her for what she'd done to him.

Two husbands…

"Quiet please," the doctor said.

"I'm sorry, but we were not told this," Mary said. "We thought we were coming to a place where there was just one man for each woman."

Could she live with two men? Have sex with both of them. Bear both of their children?

Jesse walked up beside his uncle. "This has been our way for many different reasons since Treasure Falls began. It's not a bad way to live. You have a legal husband and also a second man who would love and take care of you."

The women were all gazing at one another, wondering what to think. Should they stay or return to Charleston?

It wasn't an option for Daisy, and she knew it. Getting on that train out of Charleston had made her decision. She was committed. Though the very idea would take some getting used to.

"Ladies, I've lived this way all my life and my husbands have kept me very happy. Sadly, Silas died last year. So now it's just me and the doctor."

The tension in the room seemed to stifle the party atmosphere that had existed a few moments ago.

"Did the matchmaker not mention this?" Jesse asked.

"No," Mary said. "I'd like to know more about this way of life. I'd like to talk to Grace in private sometime. We have two weeks before we have to make a decision. I'm willing to consider having two husbands."

Daisy felt the same, though she knew she would never return to Charleston. Treasure Falls would be her life. And now she would have not one, but two husbands.

The men cheered and Jesse gave her a sweet smile.

"Me too," Daisy said.

"I will as well," Blanche said.

Slowly, the women agreed to learn more, and once again, the atmosphere changed.

"Well, then, ladies and gentlemen, let's mingle and get to know one another," the doctor said, smiling.

He moved out of the way just in time as the men came rushing toward the women. And Lee and Ellis were suddenly in front of her smiling.

"That dress you're wearing is really pretty," Lee told her, taking her arm.

"Thank you," she said and was surprised that she had no reaction to him touching her. In fact, it was like her skin warmed at the place where his fingers brushed her elbow.

"Now, I understand why the two of you were together today," she said, smiling at them wondering what it would feel like to be sandwiched between them.

Ellis took her other elbow and they guided her outside where they were still setting up the tables for dinner. Warmth flooded her in a way she had never experienced as the men walked on either side of her.

"Tell us why you became a mail-order bride," Ellis asked.

Licking her lips, she told them what Mary had said. "In Charleston, I couldn't find a single man I was interested in."

"Oh come, now," Lee said. "I'm sure the men were chasing after you. You're beautiful."

"Yes, but that doesn't mean I thought they were the right man or even nice men," she said, hoping that would stifle that inquiry.

Ellis frowned, his emerald eyes gazing at her. "What about your family?"

She swallowed. She hated lying to them, but she wasn't ready to tell them about how her father had taken Thomas's side and kicked her out of the house.

"They're dead," she said. "I was easy prey for the men of Charleston."

Ellis's brows rose, and he nodded. "I can see that. A beautiful woman without anyone to protect her."

Couples had yet to wander outside. They were alone. Lanterns were lit in the yard, casting soft light.

"You don't have to worry about that any longer," Lee

said as they pulled out a chair for her at the table. "We're here to protect you."

She smiled up at him. "Thank you."

"That is if you'll have us," he said with a grin.

They were putting her on the spot and she wasn't ready to tell them she would accept any offer.

"We'll see," she said. "I know all of us don't want to make a mistake that we would later regret."

Ellis smiled. "Agreed. We have two weeks, and I think we should take that time to get to know each other."

Lee frowned. "Why wait two weeks. Let's get married tonight and begin our journey right away."

Daisy patted him on the arm. "Lee, two weeks, and if things are going well, we'll discuss our expectations and then see what happens."

He sighed. "All right. Right now, two weeks seems like forever, but I think I can wait. As long as you let me kiss you."

This was the test. The chance to see if she would run screaming from the lovely outside area and lock the doors. This was a chance to see if she could take a man kissing her again.

Licking her lips, she smiled at him. "I thought you would never ask."

The man gave a huge grin and then he pulled her up from the chair and glanced about the area. They were alone.

"Oh, darling, you don't know how much I've wanted to kiss you since you got off that stage. If I hadn't thought you would think I was too forward, I would have done this the moment we met."

His lips slid over hers and he kissed her gently, but firmly, and then with a sigh, he released her. "If we weren't in public, that kiss would have been a lot different."

A trickle of something that she'd never felt before spiraled up her spine and she touched her tingling lips with her hand. She enjoyed the feel of his lips and she had not run screaming into the building.

She reached up and caressed his cheek. "That was the best kiss I've ever received."

And she wasn't lying. It had been wonderful.

Ellis had been watching them and she wondered about the feel of his lips on hers. After all, she would be marrying two men, not one.

Feeling unsteady, she turned to face him. "What about you, Ellis? Do you want to kiss me?"

A groan erupted from the back of his throat and he hauled her into his arms. "You're a temptress. Maybe the men back in Charleston were afraid of you?"

God, if only he knew.

"No, you make me feel brave. The two of you," she whispered.

His lips came down on hers and she loved the way his arms pulled her tightly against his body. Her arms snaked up around his neck, and she knew she could lose herself in his kiss.

Suddenly she broke off the kiss. Thomas covered her mouth, cutting off her air. She broke off the kiss, the feel-

43

ings of being smothered returning. She had to take deep breaths.

"Are you all right?" Ellis asked.

"Yes," she said. "I just became so breathless."

Oh dear, she had to somehow overcome this feeling. But it was odd that with Lee, she had not had these feelings, and yet with Ellis, she'd slipped into that darkness she wanted to avoid.

Glancing around, she realized there was only one other couple outside with them and her panic seemed to explode within her.

"I think we should go back inside," she said softly, trying to will away her fear. She could do this. These men were not Thomas, but rather two very handsome men she could be marrying soon.

Ellis was watching her and frowning. "They're about to bring the food out. Why don't we wait?"

The panic was rising inside her and she knew if she didn't get inside, she would soon be running as fast as she could.

"Why don't I go inside and bring us back some plates of food," she said. "I think it's ready."

The two men glanced at one another. She hoped they didn't think she was walking away from them because she wasn't. But she had to get inside.

"Are you feeling all right? You're pale," Ellis said.

"I'm all right. I just need a moment," she said, her feet carrying her to the house and people. She had to get away for just a little bit. She had to calm her racing heart. She had to push away the memories of what Thomas had done to her.

Lifting her dress, she moved toward the door, feeling like it was a thousand yards away and she was trudging through mud to get there.

When she reached the door, Ellis opened it for her.

"It's all right," he said. "I'm sorry. Maybe we should not have kissed you so soon."

The man was apologizing and her heart warmed. "No, it's all right. Sometimes I get overwhelmed. Give me a moment and I'll be back."

CHAPTER 8

The two men were quiet as they walked toward their home. An owl hooted and the skies were filled with stars and the shining moon. Lee wasn't certain, but he thought that something had happened tonight when they kissed Daisy.

As they strolled, the tension in the air was almost palpable.

"Did you notice that she didn't say anything about marrying two men," Ellis asked.

"Yes," Lee said. "And yet she kissed both of us."

"Maybe I was a little too forward with my kiss," Ellis said. "We were both very involved with the kiss and then suddenly she seemed to freeze and she immediately pulled away."

They continued walking.

Coyotes were singing their lonely song off in the distance. The sound always made Lee think of his family, and how they use to listen to them in the evenings.

With a sigh, he asked the question that had been bothering him all evening. "Do you think she doesn't like us?"

Ellis shook his head. "No, but something seemed to spook her while she was kissing me."

"Maybe it was the fact she was thinking about the both of us having sex with her. She just learned tonight that she would be marrying two men, not one."

"Maybe," Ellis said.

The woman was gorgeous, and for some reason, he didn't think the way she acted was a result of something they had done or said. It seemed like more.

"You're the smart one. You're the one who can always figure people out; what happened?"

Lee trusted Ellis's judgment of people and respected his opinion.

"I don't know," Ellis said. "You're just as smart as me. In fact, normally the women are the ones who flock to you, not me. But something about the way I kissed her seem to make her skittish as a newborn colt. Thank goodness she came back and had dinner with us. But I could see fear in her eyes."

Lee had also recognized that emotion in her look. He'd seen too many people in the war who had that same expression. One that they either overcame or they ran. Tonight, it seemed that Daisy had run.

"Is she still the one we want to marry?" Lee asked.

"Don't know. Let's see if she'd like to go on a picnic tomorrow. We could take her to the falls and show her around town. I'd like to kiss her again to see if she has the same reaction."

Lee thought about them being alone with her at the falls. Oh, hell, that would be so hard not to lay her down and raise her skirts and…

What if some man had taken advantage of her?

"We're going to have to be on our best behavior if we go to the falls. We can't push her or even press her. We need to take it very slow and cautious."

Ellis turned and glanced at him. "We need to talk to her about our way of life and explain to her that we will not have sex with her until we're married. We'll be tempted as hell, but it's a definite no until we say *I do*."

"Agreed," Lee said. They walked along for a few moments. "We also need to let her know that if she's lied to us, we will pull her over our knee and spank her naked ass. Something about her family didn't seem real. I think there's more to that story than she's letting on."

When they reached the steps of the house, Ellis opened the door. "She's not telling us everything. But I'm hoping that in time, she'll give us the answers we're looking for. And who can blame her? I wouldn't tell her everything about myself just yet."

Until they got to know her, there were things they would keep hidden. Things like Lee's father dying not long after his sister was born. Or things like his mother dying at such a young age and now his sister had to live alone.

"Yes," Lee said as he walked through the door. He stopped and stared around the front room, mouth gaping. The cabinet doors were hanging off their hinges, the horsehair couch had been ripped to shreds, and all the flour and sugar were strewn about the floor.

Rage filled him as he glanced about the house they had prepared for when Daisy did marry them.

Ellis stepped inside. "Son of a bitch. I'm going to kill Henry."

"This afternoon he'd been so inebriated, I would've thought he'd been asleep by dark."

Lee stared at the destruction the man had done. The drunk had done everything he could to make their home a disaster area.

With a sigh, Ellis grabbed a broom and started sweeping up the mess on the floor. Together they worked for the next two hours cleaning up the kitchen, so they could at least cook breakfast in the morning.

At midnight, they turned and headed up the stairs. "Goodnight," Ellis said as he went into his bedroom.

"Goodnight," Lee said and then he suddenly had a thought. "Wait."

Going into his room, he yanked back the sheets only to discover that the old man had slit the mattress and put brambles all over the area.

Loud cursing came from Ellis's room. "Son of a bitch, he put a snake in my bed."

They both came out of their bedrooms.

Thank goodness it was only a garter snake, but it was enough that Ellis was spitting mad. "I'm going to kick his ass. I hate snakes."

"Wait for me," Lee said, grabbing his hat and gun. Sometimes things couldn't wait until morning.

When they got to the man's home, they barged in the door.

They found him passed out on the floor. When they tried to wake him, he would just turn away from them. Finally, the two of them put him in bed.

"What do we do now? It's kind of hard to kick a passed-out drunk's ass."

"We go home," Ellis said. And then suddenly he turned toward a closed door.

Opening it, he stepped into the room. Suddenly Lee understood.

"Oh no, let's go. You don't need to be going down this rabbit hole," he said and walked into the bedroom to pull Ellis out.

The room had not been changed since Arianna's death. It still looked like a young lady's bedroom.

"Come on, let's go," Lee told his friend.

Ellis sighed and hung his head. "Son of a bitch, I'd like to kick Henry's drunk ass all the way out of town."

"Me too," Lee said. "Come on, let's go."

With a heavy heart, they walked outside into the night and began the journey home.

"Can't believe he's not changed the room. It's been over two years."

"Face it, he's never going to get over losing her."

"Sometimes I wonder if I ever will either," Ellis said.

CHAPTER 9

*D*aisy had done so well the other night until Ellis kissed her thoroughly. The memory of Thomas crushing her lips beneath his and his hands going wherever he wanted had her fighting to keep from punching Ellis. And she'd liked his kiss until the memory invaded her thoughts.

How could you banish a bad remembrance from your mind?

When would she forget about Thomas and the terrible things he'd done?

Later that day, Ellis and Lee requested to take her on a picnic, and it sounded nice, but how would they act alone with her. And could she handle two of them if they tried to do something to her?

No matter what, she could not live through another event like that. She just couldn't.

Shaking her head, a tremor of unease spiraled down her spine.

"Daisy," Aunt Grace called her. "Can I please have a word with you?"

All morning, Aunt Grace had been calling the girls in and speaking to each in private. Now it appeared it was Daisy's turn.

She walked into Doctor Owen's office. The man was out checking on a patient and Aunt Grace was using his office for their personal talks.

The office held dark furniture with one wall of medical books lining the shelves. There were instruments that she knew the doctor used in his practice and bottles filled with tinctures and pills.

"How are you, dear?"

"I'm well," she said, though she knew that last night had spooked her.

"Did you like Ellis and Lee?"

Daisy smiled. "Yes, very much. But I need to know them better before I make a decision."

She needed time to put the past behind her and to make certain she could allow them to kiss and touch her and eventually make love to her. That she could be the wife they deserved. That they were decent men who she could spend the rest of her life with.

Aunt Grace leaned back and studied her. "Many of the girls seemed uneasy with the idea of marrying two men. I was married for many years to both Owen and Silas. We were happy until Silas died. So I wanted to talk to you alone so you could ask any questions you may have."

What did she say? She didn't even understand the original sex act except that it was humiliating and painful from what she'd experienced, though the act had been interrupted and Thomas had not had time to take her virginity, thank goodness.

Maybe Aunt Grace could help her.

"You won't tell anyone my questions?"

"Of course not, dear," she said, reaching across the desk and grabbing her hands. "We're just two women talking and what we say to each other stays in this room."

Before she could stop herself, the story of what Thomas had done to her spilled from her lips. Of how her father had believed him and kicked her to the streets. The nights she spent sleeping in the bushes of the park. She told Aunt Grace everything including how she'd left a painted sign on his gate the night before she left.

The woman howled with laughter. "Son of a bitch deserved what you did. You're a survivor, Daisy. You're going to do well here."

Daisy felt tears well in her eyes. "But yesterday when Ellis kissed me, my mind filled with the memory of Thomas, and I pushed Ellis away. How can I stop this? How can I marry Ellis and Lee if I have this kind of reaction when a man kisses me?"

All night long, she'd worried about her reaction to yesterday's kiss.

With a sigh, Grace shook her head. "That's a hard one. Telling you to forget what happened is not good because you will never forget what this man did to you. But you can overcome what happened to you. Do you like Ellis? Do you like Lee?"

Things had been going so well until she reacted to Ellis's kiss. She liked both of these men.

"Oh, yes, both of their kisses were divine until suddenly my memories returned when Ellis's lips overpowered mine," she said.

When she said the words, she realized that was what frightened her, letting another man take control. Because she'd lost all control with Thomas.

"I don't know if this will work. I've never had the experience you've had, but when you start to remember, say in your mind *stop*. This man kissing me is not Thomas. He's a good man. He's the man I want to marry and I don't want my memories keeping me from being happy. I don't want Thomas to win."

Daisy tilted her head and thought about what the woman was telling her. Could it work? It was true; she didn't want Thomas to win, and if memories of his attack kept her from being happy, then he won. Already she'd lost so much because of this terrible man's actions; she didn't want to lose this new life too.

"It may not work, but I promise you that even if Ellis wasn't my nephew, I would tell you he's a wonderful man. And he will never harm you. You are safe here. He would die protecting you. And Lee is an excellent man as well."

Today, she would try this to see if it worked. Today, she was determined she was going to get over her fears of being raped. Thomas would not win again.

Staring at the older woman, she wished for just a moment that her own mother was here helping her recover instead of allowing her father to reject her. A pang of homesickness hit her and she had to take a deep breath to push it away.

"Thank you. I'm going to try to do this today when we go out on a picnic," she said. "I'm sorry to have troubled you with this."

But if it worked, she would be eternally grateful.

"No, dear, I'm glad you did. Sometimes it helps to talk about these things and I promise you no one will ever know. This will be our secret."

She had not told anyone what happened that night. Not even Mary. Though Mary knew a little from the scandal pages of the paper. But no one had heard or believed her version until now.

No one had thought about the pain of the attempted rape.

"Are you afraid of having two husbands?" Aunt Grace asked.

Daisy laughed. "I'm afraid of having one husband. Two, I can't even imagine. Please tell me that intimate relations are more fun than what I experienced that night."

"Oh, Daisy, what happens between you and your partners is wonderful. What you experienced is not the pleasure that you will find with your men. They will take care of you and make certain that you're happy. Don't think it will be anything like what happened to you before. There is no comparison."

There was so much she didn't understand. So much she had yet to learn about being with a man. A good man. Two great men.

"How does it work with two men," she asked.

For the next thirty minutes, Aunt Grace explained to her what would happen. When she told her about how they would prepare her ass and take her in both places, she gasped.

"No," she cried.

"Honey, listen to me. Once they prepare you, you'll be begging them to take you and when both men claim you at the same time. It's an experience unlike anything you've ever had before."

Daisy couldn't imagine. Her mind just couldn't comprehend how that could be pleasurable.

"All right, I'm willing to try. I can't return to Charleston, even if I wanted to."

"No, but we want you to be happy here. Maybe you should drop your family a letter and let them know you're all right. Maybe now that some time has elapsed, they are sorry for what they did to you. Your mother must be out of her mind with worry."

With a sigh, Daisy looked at her, thinking of her mother. How she'd stood at the door sobbing when her father told her to get out.

"My father has complete control of the house, and I never realized how weak my mother was until that night. My marriage will not be that way. I want to be a strong wife for my men. While they will be in control, I will still have my say. And I will die protecting my husbands and my children, especially my daughters."

Aunt Grace smiled at her. She stood and walked around the desk and hugged her. "You're going to be a fine addition to Treasure Falls. I'm so glad you're here. Don't ever forget that you are a strong woman and it's your men's job to make you happy, and yours to make them happy."

Warmth filled Daisy as she gazed at this woman who had taken them all in while they chose their husbands. She liked her a lot. Why hadn't her own mother helped her? When she had daughters, they would come to her with questions like this.

"Now, go on your picnic this afternoon and when your men kiss you, remember what I said. Tell your mind that this man kissing you is a good man who will love you and take care of you and make you happy."

Leaning back, she smiled. "Thank you for everything. Now I need to get ready. They are picking me up in thirty minutes. I want to look my best for them. I really want this to work."

Walking out the door, she turned and glanced back at Aunt Grace, the woman was wiping tears from her eyes.

For the first time since the terrible event, she felt like someone had listened to her. Someone had heard her side. Someone believed in her.

CHAPTER 10

*E*llis couldn't remember the last time he'd been so excited to go on a picnic or to spend time alone with a woman. Not since Arianna and he had secretly met at the waterfall. With a sigh, he pushed the thoughts of her out of his mind.

She was gone. For just a moment, the old ache centered in his chest. She would want him to move on.

"What a gorgeous day," Daisy said, sitting between the two of them on the bench of the wagon.

Her thigh was snug against his own and with every bump on the road, he could feel her bouncing against him. It felt good. Too good.

"Wait until you see the falls," Lee said. "They're beautiful."

"You're taking me to a waterfall?"

"Yes, it's where we get the name Treasure Falls," Lee told her.

The road out to the waterfalls was lined with pine trees

reaching to the sky. Birds flitted from the branches, calling out to one another. This was what he loved about his home. It was such a peaceful place unlike any of the cities he'd seen in the south.

"There is a legend about the falls. If you look into the water, some days you can see the reflection of someone you love who has passed this world."

Sometimes Ellis wondered if he could see Arianna. He'd glanced in the water several times, but so far, he had yet to see her face. And maybe that was for the best.

"Have you seen anyone," Daisy asked, glancing at each man.

"No," Lee said.

"No," Ellis said. He would have even liked to have seen his parents' faces, but so far nothing.

The wagon wheel hit a rut, and Daisy bounced against him and then Lee. It was going to be a long day if he kept feeling her body slam against his. Every time, his cock seemed to perk up and say *please, again.*

"Is that why it's called Treasure Falls? Because you sometimes see people in the reflection of the water?"

Lee picked up her hand and held it in his. "Once, there was an Indian warrior who loved the chief's daughter. But the chief didn't think he was the right brave to marry her. So he told the warrior if he could find the lost treasure of the Absaroka Range, he could marry his daughter. The old chief didn't believe in the treasure.

"The warrior loved the girl and he searched for months, finally, he came back and told the chief that the treasure was in the falls near Helena. The chief didn't believe him and refused to let the warrior marry his daughter. The two ran off. The chief had the warriors in his tribe go after them. When they were about to be captured, the couple confessed their love for one another and dove into the falls together. They died in each other's arms. Now you can sometimes see the faces of your dead loved ones there. The legend of Treasure Falls."

For a moment, they were all silent as they thought of the two young people dying together.

"That's sad and brave," she said.

"Yes," Lee told her. "But today, we're going to have a delicious lunch prepared by Aunt Grace's cook and spend the afternoon getting to know one another."

She smiled. "That sounds like fun."

Ellis turned the horses down the road that led to the falls and immediately the water splashing down over the mountainside into the pool below was heard. When he pulled the wagon to a stop, he glanced around to make certain they were alone.

Wildlife liked this area and he didn't want to startle a bear or a mountain lion or even an elk or a deer.

Lee stepped out of the wagon and reached back to help Daisy alight. With his hands around her waist, he lowered her to the ground.

"Thank you," she said, glancing around. "I want to peer into the water."

With a little skip, she ran to the water's edge and glanced in.

"What do you see?"

"A blonde woman staring back at me," she said with a

laugh. "She's such a lucky woman. She has not one but two men courting her. But she's not dead."

They grinned at her. Ellis liked this playful side of Daisy and hoped they would see more of it today. They had much to talk about.

A fish splashed in the pond not far from her and she giggled. "We should have brought fishing poles."

"People don't fish here, not at this pond. Someday we'll go to another pond, but not now," Ellis said, taking the blanket and the picnic basket out of the back of the wagon. He walked to where they weren't close enough to get splashed by the waterfall but could enjoy the scenery.

"Do you like to fish?" Lee asked.

"I've never been," she said. "That was not an activity that a young society woman participated in."

She walked away from the pond and sank down on the ground on the blanket that Ellis had spread. One could see from her movements, her mannerisms, and even her speech, that she had been brought up to be a southern belle. Why would she come here?

"What made you decide to become a mail-order bride?" he asked.

Opening the basket, she pulled out plates, napkins, silverware, and the food. "Oh, look she sent us apple pie. Maybe we should start with that."

Then she opened the other containers and dished out cold fried chicken, corn, and potato salad.

"Maybe not. This looks too good," she said, fixing the men a plate and handing it to them.

Ellis wondered if she was going to answer his question.

Finally, after she'd spread out the food and made their plates, she glanced at him.

"I needed to get away. After the war, the men were not the same. It was time to leave and start over."

That seemed like a reasonable answer, but was she telling the truth?

"What did your family think?"

A look of sadness filled her eyes and then she quickly looked up and smiled. "They're no longer speaking to me, but that's all right. We all must do what we have to, to survive in this world. They made their decision, and I made mine. What about the two of you? What about your families?"

Lee sighed. "My mother and father are both dead. In fact, after we eat, I'm going to look in the pond. Oh, how I would love to see their faces again."

Ellis watched her as she seemed to gather herself and smile at them. It was like she was trying not to think about her own family.

"My parents are gone" he said. "They were killed in a mining accident that took almost twenty men from town."

Her eyes widened with hours. "That's terrible."

"It was a bad time. They've been dead for at least ten years. This happened during the war. The mine was short-handed and a wooden beam gave way trapping them. By the time they were rescued, everyone was gone."

Singing came from the waterfall and they all looked around to see where it came from.

"Never heard that before," Lee said. "Maybe it's true about the spirits residing here."

Daisy gazed around. "Oh, spirits, if you're here, please bless us with your presence. We are just three individuals trying to make it in this world."

The wind rose and blew, tossing their basket. Lee jumped up to catch it before it went into the water.

"I don't think they liked that," she said.

Ellis reached over and took her hand. He pulled her closer and wiped a crumb from her lips. Her sapphire eyes widened. They were almost the same color as the water in the pond.

"That apple pie sounds awfully good right now," he said, thinking he would so much rather kiss her, but waiting, taking his time.

"Ellis," she said her voice a husky whisper. "Tell me what a marriage with you and Lee would be like."

Now they were getting somewhere. Now maybe they could explain to her their way of life.

"We would be your men. We will protect you from everything. You will never go hungry or be without a home. One of us will always be there for you. That's why we believe it's better to have two husbands rather than one."

Lee took her hand. "Understand that because we have your best interest at heart, if you don't obey us, we will spank you if you disobey."

"Spank me? I'm not a child. I'll be your wife."

"Yes, but we want you to obey," Ellis said. "We want you to trust us to take care of you."

"As your wife, I will insist you will listen to me and hear me when I'm not happy," she said. "And if we have children, you will never turn your back on them. That is not going to happen or we may as well not marry right now. I insist."

Stunned, Ellis saw her face growing red and he realized something had happened in her family life that caused her to feel this way. He didn't know what, and he hoped that eventually she would tell them.

"And you will never beat me, hit me, or force me to do something I don't agree with," she said.

Oh, yes, something most definitely had happened, but he thought they could work through it.

"Agreed," Lee said. "But again, if you disobey, we will pull you over our lap and spank you."

A frown appeared between her brows. "Can I give you the reason why I disobeyed?"

"You may, but you'll still probably receive a spanking," Ellis said, thinking they would take care of her.

She frowned. "I like the two of you, I really do, I just hope you'll be patient with me."

There was still something she wasn't telling them.

"We'll always be patient with you. We will kiss you up until the day that we marry you, but we will never have sex with you outside of marriage. We will never force ourselves on you," he said.

Tears filled her eyes and she glanced down, blinking rapidly before she glanced back at them. "Thank you."

"Let's have some of that pie," Lee said.

Quickly, he dished out the dessert, but before he gave Daisy hers, Ellis took the plate from him. He cut a bite and fed it to her. Afterward, he leaned in and licked her lips with his tongue before he kissed her.

At first, she was tense, but then she softened. Leaning back, he forked another bite and gave it to her. This time, Lee leaned in, licked her lips, and kissed her.

When he leaned back he grinned. "My favorite way to experience apple pie."

"Mine too," she said with a sigh. "Mine too."

A grin spread across her face. "Do it again, Ellis. I like it when you kiss me."

CHAPTER 11

Ten days had passed since the women arrived, and Lee and Ellis knew that their two-week time frame of getting to know Daisy would soon come to an end and they would all have to choose.

Lee's mind was made up. Daisy was their woman and he'd marry her today if she would say yes.

Ellis who was the more reluctant and had to be certain was even feeling more and more sure that she was the one.

For over the last week, they had seen her every day. Each day, she seemed to be growing more and more relaxed with them. They had learned that she was a mean card player when they played Five Hundred.

And Lee loved her laugh and giggle when she teased them when she won. Their soon-to-be wife made them happy and he hoped they were pleasing her. At least, she didn't seem as nervous as she'd been when they first met.

Every day, she laughed more, she kissed them freely, making the first move. Every day seemed better than the last, and he couldn't wait until they finally stood before a preacher and said their vows.

He was ready to claim her and make her theirs. All of his questions had been answered. All his reservations were gone. Daisy was their woman, and today, they wanted to give her something special.

They were taking her shopping.

"Are you ready for today?" Lee asked his partner, knowing that Ellis was the one holding back.

"Yes, I am," he said. "The wedding ceremony is in four days and we need to give her time to prepare."

If they hadn't been walking up to the house, Lee would have done a jig right there in the streets. "Soon we're going to be exploring her rich, full curves. My cock can hardly wait."

Ellis laughed. "Settle down, boy, we've got four more days before we say our vows. Four long days of torture while we gaze and think about what's hidden beneath her dress."

Oh, Lee knew exactly what was hidden beneath her dress. Luscious womanly curves he couldn't wait to explore. To touch her breasts, her clit, and run his tongue along her seam.

They entered the big house and saw Daisy downstairs waiting for them. When she saw them, her eyes brightened and she smiled. "Hello."

Ellis went up and kissed her on the cheek and Lee was not going to be left behind. There were other places he wanted to kiss her but would wait until they were alone.

"What are we doing today?"

"It's a surprise," Lee said, taking her by the arm. "We've got a full day planned for you."

"Oh, I like surprises," she said. "Bye, ladies."

"Bye," the other girls called after her.

The women were sitting around doing needlepoint. Lee was glad they had promised to take Daisy out today.

When they walked out into the sunshine, she lifted her face to the sun. "What a gorgeous day. How cold does it get in the wintertime?"

Ellis chuckled. "There will be snow on the ground from December to April," he said.

"And sometimes it starts earlier," Lee replied. "But don't worry, we're going to keep you warm. Already we're stock-piling wood."

Each man took her by the arm and they strolled down the street to the mercantile that Lee owned. He was excited to show her his store.

When they stopped in front of the bank, Ellis turned to her. "This is the bank I run for the family and the town of Treasure Falls."

He pushed open the door and the man behind the tellers' cage called out to them. There were two desks and a safe in the back, but it held very little money.

"Good morning, Mr. Sanders. Who is this pretty woman you have with you?"

"This is Miss Daisy Miller," Ellis said.

"Hello," Daisy called.

"Mr. Smith helps me and has been working over-time while I've been courting you," Ellis said. "Thank you."

"Glad to do it," he said. "We help each other in our community."

"See you in a couple of days," Ellis told Mr. Smith. "We've got to take her to the mercantile."

"Welcome to town, Miss Daisy," the man called.

"Thank you," she said as they walked out the door. "That was interesting seeing where you work. It's a really small bank compared to what we have in Charleston."

Ellis laughed. "I'm sure."

They walked next door and Lee pushed open the door. "Welcome to Treasure Falls Mercantile."

"Oh, look," she said, walking inside, "a store. I've forgotten what one looks like."

She strolled around the counters, gazing at the different knickknacks and canned goods for sale, the bins of coffee, flour, and bolts of material.

The man behind the counter grinned at them. Lee gestured toward his woman. "Charles, meet Miss Daisy Miller."

"Good morning, ma'am. Glad to have you in town," he said.

"Thank you," she said, her hand running over the yarn supply.

"Why don't you go to lunch. We're going to let Miss Daisy do some shopping," Lee said.

She whirled around to face him. "Shopping?"

"Yes," Lee said. "You can pick out two new dresses."

Her sapphire eyes widened and he could see the joy on her face. "Oh my. I haven't purchased anything in months."

The man behind the counter smiled and then slipped

out the door. Lee went over and turned the open sign to closed and locked the door. This was going to be a private shopping trip.

When he turned around, Daisy was crying.

"Why are you crying?" Ellis asked her.

"You're being so good to me," she said. "You don't know how badly I need new clothes."

Lee's heart filled with pride and he was glad he could provide his future wife clothing.

Ellis glanced at Lee with that worried look that appeared whenever she revealed something new.

"Before you choose the dresses, there is something else," Lee said. He walked behind the counter and pulled out a tray of rings they kept on hand. Gold wedding bands. Some even had a tiny diamond in them.

Quickly he moved from behind the counter to in front of her.

Her eyes widened and her mouth dropped open. Both men kneeled on one knee in front of her.

"Daisy Miller, will you be our wife. Will you marry us and spend the rest of your life with us?" Ellis asked.

"Have our children and stay by our side until death parts us," Lee asked, his heart pounding in his chest. This was what he wanted so badly, and he feared she would say no, even though this was what she came to Treasure Falls for.

Stunned, she stared at them, her sapphire eyes wide with shock.

"I—I didn't expect this quite so soon," she said.

"Why wait? We know you're what we want. We'll marry

with everyone else, but this would give you time to prepare," Ellis said.

She licked her lips. "I'm honored. But I'm nervous as well. Will you be patient with me? I'm a little scared about the two of you sharing me. I can't imagine having one man, but two..."

They rose and took her into their arms, both of them, sandwiching her between them. Lee loved the feel of her body between theirs.

"Darling, we'll go slow," Lee said.

"We want you to be happy," Ellis replied.

She licked her lips nervously. "Yes, I'll marry both of you."

First, Lee pulled her in close and kissed her, his lips crushing hers beneath his. When he released her, Ellis did the same, but Ellis also placed his hand on her ass and squeezed her bottom.

She jumped a little.

When his lips released hers, he stared down at her. "Darling, we can hardly wait until our wedding night."

"Daisy, we want you so badly, but we will not take you until after we say our vows," Lee said with a groan. "We promised you and we're men of our word."

They pulled her closer and let her feel how excited they were.

Lee noticed that she squeezed her eyes shut.

"Oh my," she said with a gasp. "I just hope I will make you happy."

"Which ring do you want to wear?" Lee asked. "It's your choice."

A smile flitted across her face and she shook her head. "No, you are my husbands. I want you to pick out which ring you want me to wear. They all are beautiful and will make me happy. But this is your gift to me and I want you to choose it. This ring I will someday pass down to our children."

Warmth spread through Lee. "That makes me very happy. You get to choose the dresses you're going to wear. One of them, I would like to be your wedding dress. But you get to pick the two gowns."

"Agreed," Ellis said.

She glanced between the two men smiling. "Promise me that it will always be like this between us."

They grinned. "Promise," Ellis said.

"Promise," Lee said. "Now there is one other thing you need to know. In the bedroom, you are ours. Don't choose any underwear or any underclothes because you're not going to need it after we're married."

A frown appeared on her face. "But what about when I go out in public?"

"No," Ellis said. "Nothing."

"We want you available to us, any time, any place, anywhere. Do you understand?" Lee replied. "We may decide to take you out under the stars at night or even in a field. Wherever the desire hits, that's where it's happening."

She licked her lips. "All right."

"And, darling, I promise you're going to love it," Ellis said.

They stood, staring at one another. Lee could see that

she appeared nervous once again and he wanted her to be excited and happy that they were going to marry her.

"Go do your shopping. Buy anything you need. Before winter arrives, we'll get you some boots and a coat, but right now, just get what you need. There is a dressing room behind that curtain. We want to see you try on your clothes."

"All right," Daisy said and scampered to where the ladies' pre-made dresses were hanging.

There was no dressmaker in town and Lee had a seamstress in Helena that he bought women's clothes from. Everything from dresses to long johns in the winter. Now his bride was getting to choose from his latest selection.

The two men glanced at one another and watched as she combed through the clothes.

"Which ring?" Lee asked.

"This one," Ellis said.

"Good, that's the one I wanted her to wear as well."

It was gold with roses and vines engraved in the small band.

"Shame it's not daisies instead of roses," Ellis replied.

Daisy took a handful of dresses and went behind the curtain.

"Damn, she's in there undressing," Lee said. "We could go help her."

Ellis sighed. "No, we promised her we would not touch her until after we married and we're going to keep that promise."

Lee knew Ellis was right, but that didn't make it any easier. "I just wanted a peek."

"Why? So you could walk around with your cock as hard as the rocks in the mine?"

"Yes," he said, knowing that it was true.

"By waiting, we're gaining her trust," Ellis said.

Lee knew it was true, but the waiting was making him crazy.

She came out of the dressing room and he could see she needed help. Lee all but ran to her side. "Here, let me do those buttons for you."

Gazing at her back, he couldn't wait to run his fingers along her flesh. When he slid the last button into the hole, he leaned down and kissed the back of her neck, sliding his tongue along her silky skin.

Whirling around she gazed at him. "What do you think?"

"I think I can't wait until we're married," he said with a grin.

"No, silly, about the dress. Your mind is thinking about our wedding night," she said with a smile.

"My cock is thinking about our wedding night. My mind is telling it to slow down," Lee responded.

She giggled.

Ellis came around the counter and stared at the dress on Daisy. "It's pretty. But I want to see what else you've picked out. Here, let me unbutton this dress, so Lee can gain some control."

Her brows raised. "And you're not feeling the same thing?"

"Oh, I am, but I'm a very patient man."

She grinned at him and whirled around for him to unbutton the buttons that Lee had just fastened.

Thirty minutes later, she tried on the last dress and they both nodded their approval. "Definitely this one. You look stunning in it."

She licked her lips nervous again. "Thank you for today. For the dresses and the wonderful marriage proposal I will someday tell our children about. But before you marry me, there is something you should know. Something that only Aunt Grace knows about. Something that I'm so ashamed of."

The two men glanced at one another and took her hand and led her over to a chair. She sank into the chair and began to softly weep.

CHAPTER 12

*D*aisy hadn't meant to tell them. She was never going to mention to them what Thomas had done to her, but she couldn't keep it a secret any longer. After the beautiful marriage proposal, the shopping, the way they treated her like a queen, they needed to know the truth.

Maybe they wouldn't want to marry her. Maybe they would ban her and send her back to Charleston, but it wasn't right for them not to know. To understand why sometimes she tensed or jumped or had to get away.

More than anything she wanted this marriage to work and there could be no secrets between them.

The two men sat at a table across from her. In shame, she hung her head. She had been so innocent, so naïve, and the perfect victim for Thomas.

"Four months before I left Charleston, I was the belle of the ball. In some ways, I felt like I had the world at my feet. What I wanted, I received. When I attended a soiree or ball, my dance card was always full. Until Thomas Jones began to court me. He was the son of the richest man in Charleston. The most sought after by all the debutantes and I was thrilled that he wanted me."

Closing her eyes, she tried to remember how naive she'd been. How she believed in him and never dreamed he would hurt her.

"We were the most sought-after couple in Charleston. Any day, I expected him to go to my papa and request my hand in marriage. Any day, I thought we would be announcing our engagement. Instead, I soon learned what kind of man he really was."

She thought back to that horrible night, a shiver racing down her spine, and she gave a little shake unable to ward it off. Lee picked up her hand as did Ellis.

"A woman tried to warn me, but I thought she was crazy. She must be mistaken. My Thomas would never try to be inappropriate with me or any other woman." A tear trickled down her cheek. "But she was right."

She swallowed the memory returning with a kick, like it had just happened yesterday.

"At the biggest ball of the season, he took me outside. I thought he just wanted to steal a kiss and then we would return to the party, but he wrenched my hands above my head and tied them to a tree. Then he ripped the bodice of my dress to reach my breasts. The entire time I was begging him to stop until he finally slapped me twice, nearly knocking me unconscious. Then he lifted my skirts, yanking down my bloomers."

She had to stop for a moment, the thought of what he

did next so frightening. "His hands, his fingers were every-where, and he kept telling me to stop my whining and enjoy what he was going to do to me. But I was begging him to stop."

With a deep breath, she continued. "He yanked his pants down, lifted my legs, and was about to enter me when a couple came outside into the garden and saw us."

Unable to stop herself, she began to shake.

"The man started to laugh and the woman ran in and told everyone to come outside. Thomas quickly untied my hands and pulled up his pants. In a matter of seconds, the garden was filled with curious people, including my mother and sisters who led me away."

It all seemed like only yesterday, each time she thought about that night. The humiliation, the disappointment, the way she'd gone from being the belle of the ball to nothing but a street urchin.

"My family took me home. I expected Thomas to come to our house, apologize, and ask my father for my hand. But he did not. My father went to his house and asked him what happened. Thomas lied and told him that I was the one who insisted on going into the garden and that I let him get so far that he took my virginity. That he was no longer interested in me. That I was an easy woman, that any man could take me."

Tears flowed freely down her cheeks.

"The worst part was that Papa believed him. When he came home, he immediately forced me out of the house. While my mother stood in the corner and cried, he told me that I had to leave right then. That he could not let me tarnish my sisters' good names or let my evilness rub off on them."

With a sigh, she gazed at the two men who had offered to marry her. Now they would no longer want her. Now they would send her packing.

"What did you do?" Lee asked, his face dark, his eyes flashing with anger.

"I spent the night in the park. For a week, I hid from the police, the brothel owner, and anyone else searching for me. Sleeping beneath the bushes in the park with an old blanket I found in the trash to keep me warm. Eating anything I could find. Still wearing my battered silk gown until I saw Mrs. Ida Newton, the matchmaker, putting up posters about needing mail-order brides. Then I joined her."

Ellis looked like he was ready to kill her. And Lee's face was red and filled with rage. They didn't believe her and now they would no longer want her. All their fury was directed at her for being so easy.

She had done nothing wrong and yet she was the one who continued to suffer because of what Thomas had done to her. Once again, she'd lose everything.

"Have you spoken to your family?"

"No," she said. "They don't know where I am."

"What happened to Thomas?"

Since they were going to send her home, she might as well tell them what she did with Blanche's help.

"The night before we were leaving, I painted a sign that said 'Beware Defiler Rapist. Guard Your Daughters.' That night, I went to his house and left that sign on the big fancy gate to his estate. It was a small thing, but I had to warn other women away from him."

Lee started to laugh. He glanced at Ellis who had a smile on his face.

"The next morning as we were boarding the train, the police stopped me and asked me if I had placed the sign there, and I lied telling them I was exhausted from getting ready to leave. Thank God, they let me go."

With a sigh, she stood. "I'll put the dresses back. You don't have to marry me and if you want to send me back to Charleston. I understand."

Ellis's eyes grew wide. "What are you saying? You don't want to marry us?"

Unable to stop them, the tears started to flow down her face again. "Of course, I do, but you don't want a woman who has been touched by scandal."

Lee shook his head. "If Charleston wasn't so far away, I'd go there and kill Thomas Jones for you. I'd have a word with your family about how in the world could they turn their back on you and throw you into the streets. And then I would walk you through town in the most elegant clothes. You're a lady. If you will have me, I will be your husband, protect you, and I promise no man would ever get away treating you like that again."

Warmth filled her as she gazed at Lee and Ellis.

"Thomas Jones is a dead man if he ever steps into Montana. No man is ever going to get away treating you like that again, do you understand us? You are our woman, our soon-to-be wife and, of course, we want you. What he did was sick and disturbing."

They stood and walked around the table and took her in their arms.

"Your ours. We will die protecting you," Ellis said.

"Never forget that," Lee said.

Leaning back, she stared at each man. They still wanted her. "That makes me feel wonderful."

Softly she kissed each man on the lips. "Do you remember that first night you kissed me, Ellis? Do you remember how I ran into the house?"

"Yes," he said softly. "You had a reaction that night to what had happened in your past, didn't you?"

"Yes, and that's why I'm asking for your patience. I want to give you my heart, my soul, and my body, but it may take me some time to get over what Thomas tried to do to me."

Lee softly swiped away a piece of hair that had fallen on her cheek. "Honey, we're not Thomas. We're good and decent men. We respect you. We want to give you so much pleasure. We want to hear you calling our names as you come."

His blue eyes had darkened and were soft and she knew he meant what he said.

"And no one will ever treat you that way again. Not our family, your family, or anyone else in this town. I'll kill them if they do," Ellis said.

Relief filled her as she smiled. No, she had not wanted to tell them of her shame, but they had turned her tragedy into a positive, healing experience.

While it would take some getting used to, marrying her two men would be the best thing that had happened to her in a long, long time.

"Thank you," she whispered as she leaned against them. "Thank you for choosing me. I promise to be the best wife possible."

CHAPTER 13

*I*t was their wedding day and both men had been restless all day. They were beyond excited, and after Daisy had confided in them, they both felt overly protective of their woman.

Personally, Ellis wanted to kick her father's ass right out of Charleston. Why did it seem like fathers were ignorant of their daughters' needs? Of their wants and how they needed fatherly protection? It was something Lee and he had talked about at length.

Their daughters would be the most protected women in Treasure Falls. No man would live to take advantage of their girls. And their sons would be taught to respect women. What kind of man did what Thomas did to Daisy?

Ellis was just glad that he'd been unable to take her virginity. But still, her father had been a disgrace. The thought of their woman living on the streets of Charleston was frightening.

"Stop thinking about it," Lee said, fixing his bolo tie.

"Today is about making Daisy ours. Of making her happy. Today is the beginning of our happy married life." They were getting ready to walk out the door to go to his aunt and uncle's home to marry their woman.

"I know, but I can't help but think about our children, our daughters. Even our sons will be respectful people. If not, I'll paddle their butts into next week."

Lee laughed. "First, we have to have those children. And second, you need to remember that people, particularly children, do what they want. We most certainly did."

"I know, but I never would have taken advantage of a young woman, especially one who was telling me to stop," Ellis said, thinking about Arianna. But they had been foolish and so very much in love. If her father had not interfered, he would have married her.

They closed the door to their house and walked down the street. When they returned this evening, they would be married.

With a sigh, he pushed Arianna out of his mind. That was the past. There was nothing he could do to help her now. Today was about his future.

As if conjuring him up with his thoughts, Henry Cox stepped in front of him.

"So you're getting married. You've forgotten all about my daughter."

Maybe it was prewedding jitters, but he was already nervous without having to deal with Henry.

"You kept us from marrying, remember? I came to you and asked for her hand and you said over *my dead body*. I should have killed you right then."

The man's top lip curled and he all but growled. "You weren't good enough for my daughter. Especially after she lost her brother because of your family."

"I had nothing to do with that. Mine accidents happen all the time."

"You're a Sanders, and I would never let you marry my daughter," he growled. "Never."

Ellis sighed and tried to remind himself the man was hurting. He'd lost two of his children and blamed the Sanders family for their deaths. "Look, Henry, I would do anything to bring back Arianna. I loved her. Her death weighs on me daily. I would do anything to bring back your son and my parents, but I had nothing to do with the mine accident. I lost people I loved too."

Lee stepped in. "We've got to go. We don't want to be late."

The old man stunk of liquor and Ellis knew he'd already started drinking.

"I'm going to make certain you're never happy," Henry said. "Your wife is going to be living in hell."

Before Ellis could stop him, Lee grabbed Henry by the shirt and pulled him up close to his face. "Don't ever threaten our wife. Don't even think about harming her. She had nothing to do with the death of your children, and I won't put up with your threats. Do you understand me?"

Henry's eyes grew large and Ellis could see the fear in them.

"Yes," the old man growled.

"Now get the hell out of the street. We're getting married today," Ellis said.

As they walked past him, the old man glared at them.

"Daisy doesn't deserve this," Ellis said.

"No, she doesn't. Not after what that bastard tried to do to her. But she'll be safe with us," Lee said.

"I hope so," Ellis said as they walked up to the steps of the house. This was the day they had been waiting for, for so long.

"Let's get married," Lee said. "We've got babies to make tonight."

Ellis laughed and shook his head. "You're changing the first dirty diaper."

"I can do it," Lee said. "In fact, I can't wait."

CHAPTER 14

*T*oday was her wedding day. Not the one she had imagined in Charleston of her guests being the most prestigious in the town, but rather a low-key gathering here in Treasure Falls.

And she was glad.

This felt more real. While her men had not told her they loved her, they had said they would die protecting her, and from that statement alone, she thought they loved her. She felt certain that when the time was right, they would all tell each other they loved one another.

And she was patiently waiting for that day when they all realized that their hearts were entwined and would speak of their love for one another. She could wait.

No, this was not a traditional wedding at all, but rather between her and two men. And since she arrived in Treasure Falls, she had felt accepted. Like this was where she was meant to be. Like she belonged here.

This morning, Mary and Blanche and she had sat on the

bed and asked each other if they were making the right decision and each woman agreed this was right for them. Each woman was happy with the two men who had chosen her, and each woman knew that after today, they would only see each other when they could. The months of living together were over and they were each beginning a new chapter of her life.

Daisy stood in her new yellow dress waiting for her turn to walk down the stairs, and her two men would meet her there, and once all the women were downstairs, the ceremony would begin.

Aunt Grace stood by the stairs. She hugged Daisy. "I'm so proud of you, Daisy. Good luck."

"Thank you," Daisy said, feeling the tears welling in her eyes. The woman was more like a mother than an aunt. She'd helped her overcome her fears and she would be forever grateful. Yes, the nightmare still resided in her mind, but she'd learned to overpower the pain and not let Thomas win.

Daisy began the descent and saw her two men waiting for her at the bottom. They grinned at her and when she reached them, they hugged her.

"Happy wedding day," Lee said.

"Happy wedding day," Ellis echoed. "Now you'll be ours."

She smiled at them. "And you'll be mine."

They grinned and walked her over to stand in front of the good doctor who would be saying the vows once all the couples were gathered.

Her knees were knocking, not because she doubted her

decision, but because this was such an important day in her life. Today, she chose happiness.

After they said their vows, the doctor grinned at them. "Gentlemen, you may kiss your bride."

First, Ellis leaned in and kissed her, making her knees weak. Then Lee kissed her, but he pulled her into his arms and covered her lips, molding her body against his. When he finally released her, she felt almost faint.

"Darling, I'm so happy you're my wife," he whispered as he leaned his head against her forehead.

"Me too," she said, meaning every word.

The doctor glanced at the group of them. "How wonderful. Now we know the town of Treasure Falls will continue. May you be blessed with many children and long lives together."

Afterward, they had dinner where there were toasts to happiness and well-being. The day seemed to go by in a blur, and soon, her men were taking her by the arm.

"The party is breaking up and I'm ready to go," Lee said.

"Me, as well," Ellis said, standing and glancing at Daisy. "Are you all packed?"

"Yes," she said suddenly feeling very nervous. "Let me tell the girls good-bye."

She walked over to Mary and hugged her. "Be happy."

"You too," Mary said.

Then she found Blanche who looked so excited.

"Daisy, I'm getting my dream. Another ranch. Promise me you'll come see me," she said.

"You know I will. Soon," Daisy told her. "Be happy."

"You too," she said, hugging Daisy.

Last, she went to Rose, the fourth person who had been in the stage with them. She was considered dangerous, but Daisy wasn't afraid of her.

"Good luck, Rose," she said. "I hope you find a man in Charleston."

Rose grabbed her hands. "Thank you for being my friend Daisy. It means a lot to me."

"Oh, Rose," she said, never realizing until now how much the other girls' ostracization had bothered her so much. "I'll never forget you."

"We shared a journey," she said. "I hope you're happy."

"Yes," Rose said with a shy smile.

The woman walked away and Daisy's men came up to her.

"Are you ready to go," Lee said, grinning.

The man was so eager to take her virginity. They could hardly wait to get her into bed and she was still a little nervous about being taken by two men.

"My suitcase is right there," she said, pointing to the small bag Mrs. Newton had given her before she left Charleston. "Let's go begin our life together."

Both of her husbands grinned like she was offering them candy.

She hugged Aunt Grace good-bye and the woman whispered in her ear. "Remember, every time you get nervous, say *stop, these are good men.*"

"I will," she told her and then they walked outside. Ellis had his hand on her elbow guiding her out the door.

"Goodnight, Aunt Grace," he called. "Thanks for everything."

"You're welcome," she said. "And, Lee, you too."

He turned and grinned at her and blew her a kiss.

When the couples were outside on the front porch, they separated and went to their respective homes.

The air was chilly and she realized that it was almost the fourth of July. At home, it would be hot and sultry.

"What a gorgeous night sky," she said, gazing up at the stars and the moon.

"We can go out and look at the stars any night you want to," Ellis told her.

She grinned. "I'd like to especially go out and look at the full moon. A courting moon with my two husbands."

They laughed.

When they reached the house, Lee scooped her up and she giggled. He carried her over the threshold.

"Mrs. Sanders, welcome home," he said as they walked into the house.

It was a lovely home. Smaller than her family home, but big enough for them to raise a family in. She could tell the men had made it look special just for her.

A vase full of wildflowers sat on the table and she grinned.

When Lee set her down, he let her body slide over his very hard cock. She swallowed nervously, remembering that soon, she would be experiencing both of her men.

With her hands, she could feel his rock-solid chest. His muscles were large, his arms strong. She couldn't wait to see him without a shirt and maybe even run her hands down his stomach.

Ellis came and joined her and Lee. "Welcome home, wife."

"Thank you," she said, gazing up at both of her men. "This is a lovely home."

"Tonight, we plan on giving you as much pleasure as you can take," Ellis said. "But first, there are some ground rules. Some things that we need you to understand."

"This first week, you will remain naked," Lee said.

"What? But how am I to cook for you if I'm naked," she said. "What if we have guests?"

"There will be no guests this first week," Ellis said. "People know better than to stop by."

Had she made a mistake? Was this what most married people did?

Gazing at the two men, she knew she belonged to them, and they could do with her as they wanted. She would do everything she could to fit into their lives, but this would be a tough first week.

"Tonight, your training will begin," Lee said. "We'll show you exactly what we want and how we like it. You'll be introduced to your first butt plug in order to start preparing your ass."

Ellis smiled in that naughty way that made his emerald eyes darken and sent a ripple of awareness through her. "Sometimes I'm going to spank your ass, your pussy, and maybe even your nipples. All to bring you pleasure. If it hurts, tell us. Talk to us and let us know what you enjoy and if anything bothers you. Talk to us."

That seemed fair enough, but to spank her private parts? She'd never heard of such.

"We always want to bring you pleasure," Lee said. "We also want you to desire us and give us satisfaction. So we're going to take your mouth, your pussy, and your ass, all in good time."

This was so beyond her comprehension. Sure, she knew what went on between a man and a woman, but some of this she didn't understand. Some of this was kind of frightening. But she had to trust her men.

No matter what, she had to believe they would do what was best for her.

"All right," she said. "As long as I can ask questions when I need to."

They smiled.

"Always," Lee said.

"It's time to begin," Ellis said. "Strip."

CHAPTER 15

*D*aisy had dreamed about her wedding night, but in her mind, she'd only pictured one husband, not two. Lee and Ellis had already shown her they were special, but she'd never felt so nervous.

Slowly, she unlaced her shoes, taking her time to undo the strings. Then she rolled down her stockings. Anything to prolong standing nude before them.

With a groan of frustration, Lee walked over to her. "Let me help you with the buttons on your dress."

"Easy," she said. "I don't want you to rip the buttonholes. I love this dress."

The man growled, but carefully unfastened each button. Then he moved back to stand beside Ellis who was staring at her, his eyes filled with a heat she'd never seen before.

"Daisy, can you move any faster, darling," Ellis said. "My cock is about to bust the buttons off these pants."

Licking her lips, she lowered her dress and then

stepped out of the garment. Ellis hurried to her side and undid the corset and tossed the garment into the fireplace.

"I never want to see you in this contraption ever again," he said as he kissed her bare shoulders and back. "Finish."

She untied the laces to her petticoats and stepped out of them.

Now she stood before them in her bloomers and her chemise. Knowing she would soon be bare, she took a deep breath and lifted the chemise over her head, exposing her breasts to them.

"Oh my," Lee said. "Honey, your tits are gorgeous. I can't wait to taste them."

She didn't feel gorgeous, only nervous and scared and fearful of what was about to happen. And yet, she'd known that someday she would marry and have to face her husband. Never had she imagined two men.

"Take off the bloomers," Ellis said, his voice husky as he gazed at her.

With a sigh, she slowly pulled down the bloomers, the last piece of clothing she had left on.

After she stepped out of them, she kicked them aside, but Ellis reached over and picked them up. He brought them to his nose.

"Hmm, you smell heavenly," he said with a growl. "But you won't be wearing bloomers any longer."

What women traipsed around without a corset or bloomers beneath her dress? It appeared that she would be.

Suddenly Ellis reached for her and he lifted her up and over his shoulder and carried her up the stairs. Lee followed behind him.

"A couple of rules about tonight and every night," Ellis said, dropping her on the bed.

She glanced around the room and stared at the massive bed. It was large enough for all three of them. Gazing at them, into their eyes, a calmness overcame her.

"What are the rules?" she asked.

"You will not close your eyes but look at us at all times. I want you to see we're not that man who ruined you. We're your husbands, and in the bedroom, we are in control. If something makes you uneasy, tell us, and we'll explain to you why we are doing whatever it is that makes you afraid."

"All right," she said, gazing at them. "Why am I the only one without clothes. Seems to me you should be naked as well."

This was her wedding night and she was ready to see her husbands' naked bodies. No sense in her being the only one lying here wearing nothing on.

They grinned at her and Lee began to remove his clothes as fast as he possibly could. Ellis was slower and gazed at her the entire time he was removing his boots, his shirt, and his pants.

The look on Ellis's face was one that left her feeling warm all over. It was like his gaze portrayed all the things he planned on doing to her tonight, and while part of her was excited, the other was uncertain.

Their male bodies were strong, their chests and abdomens rippled with muscles. Their arms were beefy, and their manhoods were hard and rigid. From their kiss, she knew they tasted and smelled different. Lee smelled of the outdoors and leather and horses, and Ellis tasted like he'd eaten something sweet. Both were unique. Both made her heart beat faster.

"Spread your legs," Lee commanded.

She licked her lips, her nerves once again roaring alive.

"Beautiful," Ellis said as he stroked his cock.

Before tonight, she'd never seen a man's cock before and the long member fascinated her. Smooth, rigid, and hard and she longed to touch the very end. See how it felt when he slid the skin up and back.

They kneeled on either side of her, before they lay down beside her. She knew the time was fast approaching when she would no longer be a virgin. Memories tried to control her mind, but she said her mantra over and over in her head.

Stop, these are good men. My husbands.

"We're your men, and tonight, we're going to explore every inch of you," Lee said in a soothing voice. "We're going to taste every inch of you. We're going to love every inch of you."

Lying on either side of her, she didn't know what they expected from her, but suddenly it felt like their hands were everywhere. She closed her eyes at the onslaught of feelings.

"Open your eyes and look at me," Ellis said, his voice demanding.

Fingers pinched her nipples, sending a rushing sensation through her as she opened her eyes and stared into his emerald gaze. Heat warmed her and she swallowed hard, uncertain of the feelings they were arousing within her.

Ellis took her hand and wrapped it around his cock and she gasped at the strength she could feel there.

"We're learning what makes you excited and you're going to learn what makes us aroused," Ellis said. "And, baby, I love the way you're squeezing my cock. Soon we'll have you sucking our cocks."

The thought of putting her mouth on him was strange, and she frowned.

"Let me show you what I mean," Ellis said and he scooted down the bed until his mouth was even with her pussy.

In disbelief, she watched as his tongue reached out and stroked the folds between her legs. An intense tingling sensation traveled up her spine.

She gasped. "Ellis."

"Lie back and enjoy, darling. Tonight is all about your first time and making it enjoyable."

Spreading her open, she felt his tongue dive inside her and the most delicious sensations had her grasping the quilts in her fists. Heat flooded her and a moan slipped from her lips.

"Your cunty tastes sweeter than honey," he said as he began to lick her faster, his tongue pushing up inside her, creating a spasm that had her moaning.

She felt Lee's mouth on her bare breasts as his tongue encircled her nipples and he sucked on them.

When she'd been told about how people made babies, no one ever mentioned this. The sensations, the gripping need growing inside her.

One man was at her breasts and another between her

legs doing the most sensational things to her, causing her to tense and try to escape the delicious desire that was filling her.

She closed her eyes, her breathing shallow. Thomas's image swam before her gaze; her body tensed, and she heard Lee's voice. "Open your eyes. Watch me and let me see the desire we're creating in your gaze."

When she opened her eyes, she stared into Lee's sapphire ones as his tongue laved her breasts. All thoughts of Thomas and what he'd done disappeared, and she made the vow she would gaze at her men.

Staring at them seemed to keep her demons at bay. Staring at them, she became lost in the sensations they were creating, and she felt a burgeoning sense of needing something she didn't understand.

Blood heated and pounded as it rushed through her, causing her lungs to squeeze as she gasped for breath.

Ellis nipped at her clit and she moaned

"Do you like that, Daisy?" he asked.

Part of her didn't want to admit that what he was doing to her was making her want something she didn't understand.

He slapped her on the butt. "Answer me. We want to know what you enjoy in order to pleasure you."

"Yes," she said, thinking that simple slap had sent a fire spiraling to her womanly bits.

All the heat, the fire, the inferno seemed to be building, and she clenched her fists, the urge to lift her hips overwhelming her.

"I think our wife is about to experience her first

orgasm," Lee said and he lifted her head, his lips meeting hers halfway.

This was not the gentle kisses he'd bestowed on her before. Oh no, his lips covered hers and demanded she surrender. His tongue invaded her mouth and commanded that she give in to the way his lips overpowered her own.

His hands wrapped around her jaw and held her mouth against his own as he took what he wanted from her. And she wanted him to have everything.

Desire had a stranglehold on her and she could feel the pleasure building inside ready to explode and she didn't know how to handle the feeling. Never before had she felt such intensity, all centered in her pussy and her lips.

Suddenly the world seemed to explode inside her and she moaned deep in her throat as her body tensed and shook unlike anything she'd ever felt.

Staring into Lee's eyes, she felt like she melted beneath his touch.

Leaning back, he released her lips and smiled at her. "You're so beautiful when you come."

"What happened?" she asked.

"Your first orgasm," Ellis said, rising from between her legs. "But not your last of the night."

His fingers slid inside her and she gasped.

Lee reached down between her legs and touched the little button that was nothing but nerves. His fingers slid over her folds while Ellis's fingers slid inside, twisting and preparing her.

Her heart started to race, the center of her ached, and her breathing became labored.

A fiery heat spiraled through her and she gasped. It was happening again, and she didn't understand how the desire could build so quickly.

Pleasure rippled through her and she gasped. "Ellis."

"Honey, you're dripping wet," he said. "You're ready for me to fuck you."

Lee's tongue pushed its way inside her mouth again while his fingers continued to stroke her clit. Never had she felt so many emotions at once.

So much heat.

Releasing her mouth, Lee whispered against her ear, his fingers sliding down her crack, touching her in the most private area. "We can't wait to take you here."

"Oh," she cried as his fingers circled her anus.

Lee eased his finger into her back entrance, insistent and sure. The feel of that finger probing her, swirling and demanding entry, had her moaning, raising her hips to escape the desire that ravaged her.

"Honey, I think you like my finger in your ass."

How could he say that, yet it was true. While she felt embarrassed, she'd been unprepared for the feeling of hunger, the insistent need, for him to stroke her.

"Do you like it?"

It seemed perverse, yet everything they had done to her so far, she wanted more of. She needed more.

"Yes," she whispered.

"We've waited long enough. It's time to make you ours."

"Ellis is going to take your maidenhead," Lee said as he glanced at Ellis who grinned. "I get to take you in the ass first."

Lee lay back and pulled Daisy on top of him, her back to his chest. His tongue reached out and licked her ear and she moaned. "I'm not going to take your ass tonight, but soon. And darling, I can't wait for the two of us to take you together. Your husbands claiming you at the same time, filling all your holes."

His words sent a shiver through her. The sound of his voice, the steely resolve, left her heated. There was no doubt, that eventually, they would both take her at the same time. And part of her both anticipated and dreaded that double invasion. Tonight, she was not going to think about when that would happen and how it would feel. Tonight, she needed to experience them taking her virginity.

Ellis removed his fingers from inside her and crawled on the bed over her. She was sandwiched in between the two men and she moaned at the feel of their naked flesh against her own. The strength in their bodies, their hardness against her softness.

His long, hard dick jutted out in front of him like a sword. Never had she ever considered two men, and now she couldn't imagine sex any other way. The feel of being sandwiched between them was nothing like she'd ever experienced. It was like they enfolded her into their bodies.

She felt protected, she felt cherished, and soon she would feel them inside her.

Ellis placed his rigid penis at the entrance to her pussy and suddenly fear spiraled through her.

She gazed up into his eyes and he reached out and stroked her face.

"I'll be gentle," Ellis said as if sensing her fear. "And then Lee and I are going to make you come again. And this time, I want to hear you scream. This time, I'm going to come inside you."

The words were enough to cause her breathing to increase and her heart to hammer in her chest.

A whimper escaped her before Ellis reached down, parted the folds between her legs, and rubbed the little nub there. Pleasure spiked through her and she moaned and lifted her hips as if to urge him to fuck her.

The fear melted away and she knew this was what she wanted. What she needed. That no matter what, he would make it as easy as possible for her.

Ellis moved forward and she felt him entering her pussy while his fingers continued to rub that little pleasure nub that almost had her begging him to take her.

She felt him reach the wall of resistance.

With a quick thrust, he pushed through as a sharp pain centered around the stinging area.

"Oh," she cried out.

"Are you all right?"

It was over. No longer was she a virgin. She groaned as she felt her body accommodating him, stretching to accept his long cock as he filled her.

"Yes, but you're so big," she whimpered.

"That I am," Ellis said. "And now, I'm going to make you scream when you come this time."

She gazed into Ellis's emerald eyes, wondering why she would scream. What would cause her to raise her voice, and why he would even want her to?

Slowly he began to move inside her, the friction created heat and her breathing became difficult. It was the most incredible feeling, and while he went slowly, she suddenly wanted him to hurry.

To move faster. To reach some unknown pinnacle he was carrying her to.

As soon as he was completely inside her, he pulled out and she raised her hips, needing, wanting more of him inside her, wanting to scream to put it back.

Then she felt Lee's fingers plunging inside her back entrance. With a cry, she rose and met Ellis and then back down on Lee's fingers. Oh God, she wanted more. Up and down, she rode them, seeking the pleasure they were bringing her.

Moans filled the air and she realized this was what he meant by wanting her to scream. Her blood was pounding, rushing through her toward some destination that she knew would bring fulfillment.

Lee whispered against her ear, his breath warm and tingly. "That's it, sweetheart, open up for me. Take me inside your ass. Let me fill you while Ellis fills your pussy. Let us both give you pleasure."

And they were. Never before had she felt such heat and fire building inside her. Lee pushed a second finger inside her bottom and she squealed at the pain and pleasure exploding inside her. She could feel them going back and forth inside her body, the heat building, the fire raging, and she felt her orgasm roaring toward her.

"Ellis," she screamed as she clenched his cock inside her tightly, squeezing it. Waves of desire filled her, and for a moment, she felt like she would drown as she gulped for air.

He exploded inside her, coating her pussy walls with his seed.

Lee held her body as she shook and jerked, the passion cresting, returning her to earth, spent.

Sagging against him, she felt amazing. Better than she could remember she'd felt in a long time. She was safe. She was warm. And more than anything, she knew her husbands would protect her.

Lying there, so relaxed, she gazed up at Ellis. "That was wonderful."

He grinned. "We're not finished. You need to take care of Lee."

With a smile, she turned to Lee.

"Can you do better than that?"

He laughed. "Oh no, we've created a delicious monster. It's not a matter of better, but different."

"Up on your knees. I want to take you from behind. I want to spank that delicious full ass of yours. I want to shove my cock in your sweet cuny while my fingers stroke your ass. So yes, you better be ready."

His words were rough and yet they left her longing, wanting more. Heat spiraled through Daisy and slowly she rose to her knees.

Lee moved behind her with Ellis beneath her. Looking back at Lee, he rubbed his hand over her buttocks, creating a warmth. "Sorry, darling, but I want to hear you moan."

Slap! He hit her buttocks with his hand.

Shock and a stinging sensation rippled through her all

the way to her pussy. Heat seared her ass and yet it was a delicious warmth that left her wanting more. "Lee."

"One more time," he said as his hand connected with her ass. It burned but the heat created a fire inside. A fire that centered in her middle.

With a sigh, he pushed her forward until her head rested on Ellis's chest, her ass sticking up in the air.

"Now that's the sight I've been waiting to see. Your cheeks slightly pink from my hand, your pussy dripping with want for me, and your ass just begging for my finger."

Moaning, she glanced back at him and blew him a kiss. It seemed to spur him on as he plunged into her waiting cunty.

A groan escaped from her, not from pain, but pleasure as Ellis's lips consumed hers while Lee hammered into her pussy. This was no gentle fucking, but rather, he was showing her a rougher kind of sex.

And strangely she liked it even better than the first time.

As Ellis's kiss commanded her surrender, his lips ravaged her lips, his tongue demanding entry, his fingers twisting her nipples. Oh, how she loved the way Ellis kissed and the way Lee slammed his cock into her again and again.

Needing to draw as much air into her lungs as possible, Daisy felt another orgasm building within her.

The bed squeaked, the mattress hitting the back wall as Lee pounded into her over and over.

"Don't come," he commanded and she wondered how he thought she could hold back. The need was building, roaring through her, and at any moment, she knew she would tumble over the edge.

"I can't…"

Smack, he hit her ass with his palm and lifted her hips to meet him. A scream built inside her that she knew would soon be released.

"Do it again."

Smack, he hit her ass again and the orgasm rushed at her and she knew there would be no holding back.

"Now. Now, you can come," he cried as his seed exploded inside her womb, coating her pussy walls.

A scream tore from her throat. "Lee. Oh, Lee."

Ellis held her against him while she writhed and convulsed in his arms. Finally, they collapsed onto the bed. Totally spent, she lay there knowing she would never be the same.

Knowing she truly belonged to Ellis and Lee.

Exhausted, Lee and Ellis arranged Daisy until she lay between them.

"This is how it will always be. You between the two of us. Whenever we're in the bedroom, you will be between us."

"You're ours," Lee said. "Never forget it. You belong to me and Ellis."

How much luckier could a woman get than to have two men who looked out for her in her bed every night. Two men who introduced her to the joys of sexual pleasure. Already she wondered when they could do it again.

CHAPTER 16

*T*his morning when Lee awoke, he realized he was a married man. The smell of sex and woman overwhelmed him as the memories of his wedding night came rushing back.

The long wait of finding a wife had been well worth it. The men in Charleston were stupid to let such a beautiful, tempting woman get away.

And her family were idiots to think she wanted that toad's advances. Here in their arms, she would be protected.

Daisy had been better than any woman he'd ever fucked. And this morning, he planned on starting his day off with her in his arms and his cock between her legs.

Ellis rolled over, stretching, nude and smiled at Lee.

"Damn, was it really that good last night?"

"Yes, and this morning is going to be even better," Lee said.

Ellis slipped his fingers between her legs and pulled them apart. She moaned in her sleep.

"I think she's dreaming of us," he said. "She's wet."

Unable to wait a moment longer, Lee kissed her lips trying to awaken her. Last night had convinced him that marrying Daisy had been the best decision the two men ever made. Thank God those fools in Charleston had sent her packing. Thank God she had arrived on their doorstep.

All it took was one night and he'd become besotted with Daisy.

He trailed his lips across her lips, down her neck to her shoulder where he lightly bit her.

She moaned and opened her eyes slowly.

"Good morning. It's time for you to learn to suck my cock."

Last night, he had not taught her what he enjoyed the most. This morning, she would soon learn the finer techniques of sucking a man's cock. And he couldn't wait to get started.

"What?"

He rolled her over, so he was underneath her as he sat up against the headboard of the bed. Teaching his wife to suck his cock would start off any day the right way.

"Put your lips around my cock and suck on the head," Lee commanded. "Just like Ellis licked your pussy last night."

He pulled her head down to his cock and she opened her mouth. With a sigh, he felt her sweet lips touching the bulbous head and had to resist the urge to shove it as deep as he could. All in good time, but for now, he needed to go slow.

After all, their wife was just learning, but he knew that soon, she would be excellent at sucking cock.

"Now run your tongue around it and suck on the bulb," he said with a moan.

As she sucked on Lee's cock, Ellis moved behind her. His fingers teased her clit.

A moan escaped and Lee jerked at the vibration that surrounded his organ when she moaned. That sweet vibration left him even harder.

"Twist her clitty again," he instructed Ellis. "Darling, you're doing a great job. I like the way your mouth vibrated when you moaned."

Ellis thrust his fingers into her pussy and she groaned all over Lee's cock. Laying his head back against the headboard, he watched as Ellis spread her cheeks before he placed his mouth against her pussy.

This time, her moan was even deeper, and Lee had to concentrate on the way her tongue swirled around his cock or he would have come right then. And he wasn't ready to come the first time. He wanted to draw this out as long as possible.

"Darling, yes, like that. Suck on the head. Oh, that feels good," Lee said, knowing if they kept this up, he wouldn't last much longer. The sensations of her reactions to what Ellis was doing were rushing his climax toward fruition.

She moaned around him and his hands slid into her hair as he could feel the gathering of his seed, the rush coming right at him. Oh, how he wanted to hold back but knew that was impossible.

"I'm going to come," Lee said as he lay back and angled her mouth to receive him.

Ellis's hands gripped her hips as his tongue worked its magic on her clit. She began to thrash her body, needing, wanting what they could give her.

Lee grabbed her head and pushed his cock farther in her mouth as he moved her head up and down using her hair to guide him, enjoying the feel of her lips as they sucked him.

"I'm going to come in your mouth, Daisy. Swallow it all," he said as he groaned, his body going rigid as he shoved his cock deeper into her throat. His orgasm rushed toward him like a herd of stampeding cattle, and with one last shove, he knew he was coming.

"Daisy," Lee cried, his seed filling her mouth. "Dear sweet Daisy."

The woman was learning and she swallowed every drop before she leaned her head on his chest.

"Ellis, please," she cried, glancing back at him over her shoulder as he pulled his mouth away and moved behind her. She leaned back, eager to receive his cock.

"What do you want, darling?"

How quickly after last night she had gone from being a sweet innocent virgin, to such a tempting seductress. Her sapphire eyes darkened with passion as she glanced behind at Ellis.

"You, please, I need you," she cried.

This was how it should always be between them. The

passion, the desire, the need for each other, and Lee could already feel his cock starting to harden once again.

He watched as Ellis slammed into her pussy with his rock-hard cock and she groaned. For a moment, they moved in unison as he held her hips, rocking her exactly like he wanted.

Someday soon, he would be taking her ass. Someday soon, she would be between the two of them as they claimed her. And he couldn't wait to experience the two of them taking her at the same time. Making her theirs.

Reaching for her breasts, Lee twisted her nipples and she gasped. While he played with her breasts, he watched his friend push his fingers into her back passage.

"Ellis," she cried, her voice almost urgent with her need.

"Stop," Lee said.

Ellis halted and Lee tipped her chin up to stare into her beautiful sky-blue eyes.

"What do you think, beautiful? Should we continue or are you ready to get up and start the day? Remember, you're going to be naked and available to us all day."

A whimper escaped from between her lips.

"What do you want? Do you like Ellis fingering your ass? Do you want him to continue?"

She glanced behind her at him and Lee knew she didn't want to admit it. And he was determined that she get over her insecurities, her fears.

"Be honest with us," he whispered against her head. "Or I'll turn you over my knee and spank your white ass until it's pink. Do you understand?"

"Yes, it feels good," she moaned and stared at Lee. "You're making me into a wanton woman."

Lee laughed. "Yes, we are. But only for us."

"Yes, do that," she cried as Ellis began to stretch her even farther with a second finger.

"Relax and let me in. Soon we're going to take you back here," Ellis promised. "Soon I'm going to shove my cock so far up your ass, you'll be seeing stars. Who do you belong to?"

"You and Lee," she cried.

Lee covered her mouth with his as Ellis plunged three fingers into her and she moaned in his mouth. He loved how overnight she had become their woman. Their wanton woman.

She released Lee's mouth. "I'm going to come."

"Not yet, darling," Ellis said, and he slapped her ass, not once, but twice.

"Ellis," she cried as she bit her lip. "If you do that again, I'm not going to be able to stop."

"And then I will punish you," Ellis said, leaning up next to her ear. "Grip my cock with your pussy."

"Oh," she cried.

"Yes, just like that. Squeeze me dry. Milk my seed into your body."

Lee watched as his friend pounded into her pussy, his cock plunging in and out.

Opening his palm, he slapped her again on the ass. "Now, you may come."

"Ellis," she screamed, her body tensing as Lee wrapped

his arms around her as she spun out of control. "Oh, please."

She screamed with pleasure, her body shaking and undulating as the orgasm rocked her over and over while Lee held her.

Daisy belonged to them and no one would ever take her from them and live to tell the tale.

Ellis and Daisy collapsed onto the bed. The two men moved her until she was between them again. This time they were on either side of her while they lay in silence as they caught their breath.

"What a way to begin the day," Lee said, smiling from ear to ear.

Ellis grinned, stood, and walked to a dresser nearby. He opened the drawer and pulled out a razor and cup.

Lee pulled her until she was resting in his lap and he gently spread her legs. He couldn't wait to see her bare. To be able to kiss that sweet pussy of hers without anything coming between him and her sweet flesh. He couldn't wait to walk up to her, bend her over, and slide his cock into her bare pussy.

"We're going to shave you, and then we'll give you your first butt plug. Do you know what a butt plug is?"

"Yes, Aunt Grace told me that you would use it to prepare me. But shaving?"

Lee leaned down and kissed her. "We want that pussy to be shining. To touch your sweet flesh without anything coming between us. To slide our cocks in without your hair being in the way."

"Oh. So you're going to shave my lady parts?"

"Yes," Ellis said and dropped the lather onto her mound. With the first brush of shaving cream, she moaned.

"That tickled me down there," she said.

The men looked at each other and smiled.

"Ellis," she said, her voice nervous as he raised the razor just above her.

"I would never hurt this pussy."

"Relax," Lee told her. "You're going to enjoy being shaved."

Her fingers gripped the cotton sheet and she moaned as the bristles of the brush swept across her mound, tickling her clit. Her hips raised instinctively toward the brush.

Ellis swept the razor across her mound, his fingers steady as he cleared the hair and her sweet mound shined in the morning sun.

"Oh, darling, we may have to satisfy you again," Lee told her. "Does it feel good?"

"Yes," she cried.

She glanced down at her folds. "It's bare."

"Yes," Lee told her.

"Now for the butt plug," Ellis said, rising from the bed and going to the dresser once again.

"Up on your knees," Lee demanded. "With your head down on your arms and your ass in the air."

Lee watched as his friend pushed something gooey into her ass and then spread her hips, exposing her back passage.

"Soon, you won't need a butt plug. Soon, you'll be taking us both at the same time. I can't wait to shove my cock in your ass. For both of us to claim you at the same time. Then you'll truly be ours."

A whimper came from her.

"Don't make me spank you. Relax."

The sight of her ass spread as Ellis prepared her made Lee's cock spring back to life.

"Hurry, I want to fuck her," Lee said, the desire overwhelming him at the sight of her ass sticking up in the air as Ellis pushed the butt plug in.

That pearly white ass of hers quivering with anticipation as he pushed in the wooden dowel made Lee desire her. Now.

"Oh," she cried. "Please."

"All in," Ellis said and gave her a smack on the ass.

"Aargh," she cried. "I felt the vibrations all the way through to my pussy."

Ellis grinned. "Don't tempt me to do it again. Sometime today, I'm going to smack your ass just to give you pleasure."

"Oh," she cried.

"Roll over on your back and spread your legs," Lee commanded, his need urgent. "I'm going to shove my cock into your sweet pussy, so that you can experience both the plug and me at the same time. And, honey, I'm not going to be gentle."

"Oh," she cried as she rolled over and spread her legs.

The sight of her bare pussy as she gazed up at him, her sapphire eyes dark with passion, made him rock hard.

"I'm going to pound that sweet pussy of yours."

He pushed his cock into her shaved pussy.

"It's too much," she groaned, clenching the bedsheets. "It's so tight."

There was no way, he was going to take out the fullness that made her even tighter as she gripped his cock. That was part of the enjoyment and she would soon stretch to accommodate both.

"Honey, I promise, you're going to enjoy Lee fucking you with the butt plug in. It will be all right," Ellis told her, stroking her face.

She took a deep breath and Lee noticed that her sapphire eyes grew large with passion and her upper lip curled like she was fighting to keep from coming.

"All better," he asked, knowing he wouldn't last much longer. Her pussy was just so tight and gave his cock so much pleasure.

Ellis reached down and sucked her breast into his mouth. She gripped the sheets. "Ellis."

"Darling, is there something you need?"

"Oh yes, please, Lee, hurry," she gasped. "I don't think I can hold off—"

Ellis leaned back, but kept his fingers on her nipples, twisting them.

Lee raised her legs over her shoulder as he pounded into her pussy and then he smacked the butt plug, not once but twice.

She squeezed his cock, pulling him deep inside her.

A shudder rippled through them both. "Daisy."

"Lee," she screamed as she came all over his cock.

With one last shove, he flooded her pussy with his seed. With another shove, felt his body relax.

As he lowered her legs, he slumped over her body.

"What a way to start the day," he said with a grin.

They lay there for a couple of moments resting. Today was the beginning of their life together and he was so excited. Daisy was theirs and never would he give her up. Today, they might just keep her in bed between them all day long.

With a sigh, he rolled over and pulled her into his arms.

"So what do you think of married life so far," Ellis asked her.

A smile spread across her face. "I'm the luckiest woman alive. Not one husband, but two. What more could a woman want?"

Lee grinned at Ellis. Finally, he was getting what he wanted. A wife, and hopefully soon, a family. A couple of babies that would look like their mother. A family to replace what he'd lost.

CHAPTER 17

a week later, Daisy was back to wearing dresses, but without any bloomers beneath her skirts. And almost every evening when her men walked in the door, one of them would raise her skirts, bend her over the table or a chair and soon have her moaning.

Quickly she had learned to have supper ready for them because afterward she would be like a limp rag until they carried her upstairs to bed for the evening. There, once again, they would have her spread beneath them.

They seemed to take turns trying to see who could get the most reactions from her. Every evening, she was ready and waiting by the door for them, their supper on the table.

Thank goodness, her mother had insisted that her daughters learn to cook, even though they had servants in their home who prepared the meals.

This afternoon, she gazed about her new home and felt blessed. Thank goodness, Mrs. Newton, the matchmaker, had taken her in and sent her to Treasure Falls. Yes, some of the women had been unhappy that she didn't tell them what they were getting into, but Daisy was glad.

This way, she didn't have three months of traveling to think about how two men would be sharing her. This way it was a total surprise and she had no choice in the matter.

Her new life here was the best thing that had ever happened to her, and she knew she was falling in love with her husbands. Ellis's dark sexual glances let her know he wanted her. Lee's bright bubbly personality that quickly turned into him needing to fuck her. Both men made her happy. Both men knew how to have her screaming their names.

With a sigh, she realized how much her life had changed for the better.

Since the wedding, she'd been thinking of writing her sisters to let them know where she was and to warn them to stay away from Thomas Jones. He was a dangerous man, and the thought of one of them suffering what she had experienced frightened her.

For the first time since the incident, she felt safe and didn't fear that Mr. Jones could retaliate against her in any way. Her men would never allow him to harm her. He would do well to stay out of the state of Montana.

But her sisters were vulnerable.

So this morning after her men left, she sat and wrote her sisters a letter. Not her mother or her father, but her dear sisters who she missed so very much.

With a quill and an ink well, she found some paper and began.

Dearest sisters,

I hope my letter finds you doing well and that the scandal did not harm you in any way. Again, I would tell you that I'm innocent, but Papa made his decision very quickly, and I've accepted that I will never see any of you ever again.

After sleeping on the streets for almost a week, a woman took me in and sent me to Treasure Falls, Montana, as a mail-order bride. Yes, I'm married and I must tell you, I'm very happy. My husband is wonderful and he's taking great care of me. My life has become happy and the little town of Treasure Falls is beautiful. There are mountains and pine trees and my husband runs the local bank.

But I'm worried about you, dear sisters. Please do not have anything to do with Thomas. Do not let yourselves be alone with him. Avoid him at all costs. For if you do, you will suffer the same consequences I did. And I have every reason to think he has gotten away with this more than once. Don't be his next victim.

I would love to hear from you but understand if you think it would be scandalous of you to speak to me again. Just know that in the end, Mr. Jones did not win nor did Papa. I won by getting myself out of a horrible situation.

I'm here in Montana, happily married and hoping that soon we will start our family. Take care and know that I truly miss you, but I will never return to Charleston. Too many bad memories are there and I'm happy here with Ellis.

Love,

Daisy

While she knew she could have told them that she married two men, she didn't want to upset them. They would not understand the pleasure of two men taking care of her. Even the need for two husbands.

Now she couldn't imagine it any other way.

With a sigh, she wrote the address on an envelope and sealed the letter inside. Maybe tomorrow, Lee or Ellis could mail it for her.

No matter what happened in Charleston, she felt better that she had warned her sisters of the danger of Thomas Jones. She felt like she had done her duty.

With a sigh, she watched her men walk up the porch of the house. They were home early and she could just bet that they came home to fuck her.

CHAPTER 18

*A*bout once a month, a pony express rider would come to town with letters and correspondence for the citizens of Treasure Falls. Today when he arrived, Lee handed the man Daisy's letter to her sisters, but he'd been shocked when he received a letter from his sister's friend.

Occasionally, Beth wrote and asked for money. The girl was not married and had a hard time holding down a job. Lee wished she'd find a good man and settle down and have a couple of children. But so far, nothing.

Already he was sending her one hundred dollars a month.

He slit open the letter, fearing that it would say that she had passed.

Dear Mr. Chapman,

I'm your sister Beth's friend and I'm writing to tell you I'm worried about her. George Richards, a very wealthy man here in town, is courting her. But it's rumored that he is abusive to women. The last two women he courted, disappeared and were never seen again. This concerns me that Beth would consider him.

It's also rumored that he keeps women at the Gold Mine Brothel. I've not seen Beth in a week and I hope she's not working there because of Mr. Richards. Please come to Helena and find her.

This is none of my business, but I wanted you to know in case she disappears.

Sincerely,

Katherine Johnson

Fear spiraled through Lee. His only sister was in danger. He looked at the date of the letter. A week ago. Even now she could be missing or dead.

The door opened and several customers entered the store, but he continued to stare at the letter in his hands. Surely, Beth would not be working at a brothel. Surely, no man could convince her to take up the trade.

As much as he hated going off and leaving Ellis and Daisy, he had to go to Helena. It was only about a four-hour ride on horse, but he had no choice. He would convince her to return with him to Treasure Falls where he could watch her. Take care of her.

Glancing at his watch, he knew it was too late to leave today. But first thing in the morning, he would be riding toward Helena. An ache gripped his heart. Oh, how he wished his family was closer. Beth was all he had left.

And now she was in trouble.

He glanced at his helper. "Here are the keys. You open

and close whenever you need to. I've got to go to Helena to take care of a family situation. Watch over the store."

"Yes, sir," Charles said, gazing at him. "Safe travels."

Lee waved good-bye as he walked out the door and went into the bank next door. Ellis glanced up at him with a frown on his face.

It wasn't often that Lee came to visit the bank. Usually, they met on the wooden sidewalk when the day was done.

"What's wrong? Is Daisy all right?"

With a sigh, he walked up to Ellis and sank down behind his desk. He reached into his pocket and tossed him the letter from Katherine. His friend frowned as he opened the envelope and took out the letter. Quickly, he scanned the contents and then looked up at Lee, a frown between his brows.

"Not good," he said. "What are you going to do?"

"I'm going to go to Helena tomorrow morning."

Ellis shook his head. "This man is powerful and rich. You don't need to tangle with him by yourself. We'll both go."

"And leave Daisy alone?"

"Yes," Ellis said. "She'll be fine."

Standing, Ellis glanced at his helper. "Let me tell Mr. Smith that we'll be gone for a few days."

Lee didn't like the idea of Daisy being left behind, especially with Henry causing problems. Somehow he had to convince Ellis to stay behind.

An hour later, they walked up the steps to the house. They were home early and as Lee glanced in through the door, he could see Daisy in the kitchen preparing their dinner. Her long blonde curls hung down her back and he loved her pert little ass as she bent over checking the oven.

They opened the door and stepped inside, she came rushing to the kitchen door.

"We're home," Ellis called.

"You're early," she said, gazing at them suspiciously.

Ellis walked in and kissed her on the cheek, took her hand, and led her to the couch.

"What's wrong?"

Her sapphire eyes darkened with suspicion and fear.

"We've got to make a trip to Helena," Ellis said.

"No," Lee said. "I'm going alone and Ellis will stay here with you. I don't like the idea of you being alone."

Ellis shook his head. "And I don't like the idea of you going up against a powerful man alone."

"Someone needs to stay here and protect Daisy," Lee said. "I don't want her by herself with Henry being all crazy."

For a moment, Ellis didn't say a word, but frowned at Lee and he knew he was considering what he had said. Henry was crazy.

"Who is Henry and why are we going to Helena?" Daisy asked, standing, her hands on her hips. "What are you not telling me? We agreed to no secrets. I told you about Thomas."

Lee could see the fire flashing in those sapphire eyes and he realized they had told her very little about their pasts. The entire time they courted, they had played and had fun, but nothing serious had ever been discussed.

She deserved to know the truth.

He pulled the letter out of his pocket and handed it to her. "I received this today. Beth is my sister."

Her eyes widened and she shook her head. "You have a sister and you never told me?"

"Yes. She lives in Helena and may be in trouble."

Daisy turned and walked into the kitchen. They could hear the pots and pans being banged around.

"I think she's mad," Ellis said.

"Why?" Lee asked, staring at his friend.

"I could be wrong, but I think it's because you didn't tell her about your family," Ellis said. "I think she misses her sisters something fierce. That's why she wrote them a letter."

Suddenly she was back in the room, standing before them. "If there are any other secrets, you need to tell me now. And who is Henry?"

Ellis sighed. "Henry is the drunk in town who hates me. His son died in the mine and he blames my family for his death."

She frowned and Lee could see her thinking about his response. Ellis should come clean about it all, but so far he hadn't. It was hard to talk about Arianna and he didn't want to explain to her how he let the old man convince him not to marry her.

"But you're not in charge of the mine. That's your brother and Andrew."

It was true. The woman was not stupid. In fact, she was damn smart.

"I know, but drunks don't often think logically."

Lee had to turn his head. Why didn't he just tell her the

truth? Sooner or later, she was going to learn the truth and then she'd be furious at Ellis for not being honest.

With a sigh, Lee stood and stretched. "What if we all go to Helena? Daisy has never been, and this way, we could keep an eye on her and you'll be with me when I confront this man about my sister."

Daisy stopped and gazed at the two men. He could see she was interested in going. He could see the excitement growing in her eyes.

"If I get pregnant, I might not get another chance anytime soon. This would be a good time for the three of us to go together."

Ellis smiled and nodded. Lee knew he was just glad they were off the subject of Henry Cox. But this would not be the end of it, and when Daisy learned the truth, she was going to be furious at him.

"How far away is it?" she asked.

"Five hours by wagon, and we will go by wagon, so that hopefully, my sister will return with us," Lee said.

"Yes, let's take the wagon, so we can pick up some extra supplies."

A smile spread across Daisy's face. "So we're all going tomorrow?"

"We're all going," Ellis said.

Her eyes all but danced as she flounced toward the kitchen, then glanced back at them. A frown appeared between her brows. "Now, I don't have to be angry at you any longer. But there had better be no more secrets."

After she walked into the kitchen, Lee turned to Ellis. "Why didn't you tell her about Henry and Arianna?"

He sighed. "It's hard to talk about. No matter what, I'll always love Arianna and the child she carried. It's just Henry I can't stand. The man brought all of this heartache on all of us. He was the one who stood in the way of us marrying."

"Don't let him ruin what you have with Daisy. If she finds out from someone other than you, she'll be angry."

"I know, but I just haven't wanted to talk about it. Someday soon, I'll tell her."

"You better and I wouldn't wait too long."

CHAPTER 19

*I*t was dark when they pulled into Helena. Daisy sat between Lee and Ellis on the hard bench of the wagon as she gazed about at the small town. It was much bigger than Treasure Falls, but nothing compared to Charleston.

The main street in town had two saloons, three brothels, two mercantiles, a dressmaker, and so many other little shops, like bakeries, five and dimes, and specialty shops. Everything that Treasure Falls was missing and yet Daisy knew she wouldn't trade where she lived.

"Where are we staying the night?" she asked.

"We're going to check in at the hotel, and then Ellis and I are going to the brothel," he said.

She knew it was not a place where women went, but after her initiation into sex, she was curious. "Why can't I go?"

"Because this is not an appropriate place for a woman," Ellis said. "Especially our wife."

"But it's a place my husbands should be allowed to visit without me?"

The two men glanced at one another and frowned. They hadn't considered how she would feel with them going into a brothel. Sure, she had no doubts about them, they were good men, but still, no woman wanted her man to be tempted.

Glancing back down the street, she turned and gazed at her husbands. "So you're going to leave me alone in the hotel. I'm supposed to just sit there and wait for you while you go to a brothel and are tempted by women."

"Don't worry, we know what we have. We won't be tempted," Lee said.

The two men glowered at her.

"When I get bored, I often get into trouble," she said. "And this city has so many places to explore. So many temptations. There is the dressmaker's shop, several mercantiles, saloons, and other exciting shops. One looked particularly interesting. What is a fine dining club for gentlemen? Why is it just for men?"

Ellis began shaking his head. "Never go in there. That's where wealthy men dine and often meet with ladies that their wives don't know about. That's where they take their mistresses."

She tilted her head and raised her brows. "A cheating husbands club. Lovely."

"Yes," Lee said.

Placing her finger on her lips, she bit her bottom lip and tilted her head with a saucy smile on her face. "All right. You can leave me behind at the hotel. I'll find something to keep myself entertained with while you're gone. I've never been in a saloon. Maybe that's where I should go."

Both men at the same time said, "No."

She giggled. "Well, where is a woman to go to be entertained?"

A groan escaped Lee and he shook his head. "All right, you can go to the bordello with us, but you will wear a mask and not say a word. Do you understand me?"

A grin the size of Texas spread across her face. "Thank you."

Ellis turned and shook his head.

"You give in way too easy," he said to Lee.

"I'm not willing to find out what kind of trouble she could get into while we're gone. At the bordello, we are in control."

"That's what you think," Ellis said.

Daisy giggled, but she didn't say a word. She'd gotten her way and now they would not leave her alone. Besides, she wanted to see what she escaped.

After they dropped off the wagon at the stables, they walked down the street and found a hotel for the night. Then they had dinner. Finally, it came time to see if they could find Lee's sister. Daisy dearly hoped they would not see her working as a whore.

Lee would be devastated and she didn't want to see her husband hurt.

The men covered her face with a scarf that hid everything but her eyes. She could barely breathe as they entered the place. A piano player was banging out a song on an old piano. The noise was deafening.

Dear God, she'd gotten so lucky.

When they walked in, the madam pulled them aside. "No women are allowed unless you're taking her upstairs."

The older woman didn't smile, and in fact, she looked mean as hell. Like she could shoot to kill, step over the body, and continue working. No questions asked.

"We are," Ellis told the lady. "But we're going to need a room with a peephole. We want to see what's going on in the rooms next to us. And even the downstairs room if you have one."

The woman smiled and took their money and then led them up the stairs.

Daisy was so busy trying to see everything that was going on. There was a bar where men sat drinking. There were scantily clad women walking around the room, whispering in men's ears, and one lady wore a dress that was tied at the waist. Whenever a man said something to her, she would open her dress and expose herself to him.

"Oh my," Daisy said.

"Are you going to ask the madam about Beth?" Ellis whispered when the madam couldn't hear him.

"Not until we look around. I'm afraid she'll throw us out if Beth is working here. I just hope to God, she's not here."

When she walked in the door of the bordello, she couldn't help but remember how the man had followed her about the streets, trying to capture her and put her to work in Charleston. But she'd outsmarted the man. And thank God, she had.

This could have been her life.

At the top of the stairs, the madam took a key out and opened a door. "One hour."

"Yes, ma'am," the men said and pushed Daisy inside.

The room was small and only held a small bed.

"Strip," Ellis said.

Stunned, she stared at him. "Why?"

"You wanted to be here and now you're going to get the full experience," he said.

Lee laughed and walked over to the peepholes. "I hope I don't see Beth here. That would be awful."

"How could you see her?" Daisy asked, removing her shoes and stockings.

"This is a peephole. When you move the covering, you can see into the room next to you. Come here."

Daisy couldn't imagine seeing someone you knew having sex. Nervous, she stepped over to Lee.

"Look right through here," he said

She glanced in and was shocked at the sight. A man was behind a woman and he had her face down on the bed, with her ass sticking in the air. With his hand, he was spanking her. The girl was crying.

"Are you going to disobey me again," he asked.

"No," she cried. "Please fuck me. I need you to make me come."

"I'm going to shove my cock in you so hard," he cried out as he began to push into her.

The woman moaned as he entered her from behind.

"More."

Reaching out to her waist, he pulled her up hard against him. "Is that enough for you?"

"Yes," she cried.

Daisy could feel her own body becoming aroused.

"Do you like what you see?" Lee asked.

"Yes," Daisy whispered, unable to stop looking.

"Then why is your dress still on?" Ellis asked. "Didn't I tell you to remove it?"

She turned from the sight of the man and woman. Turning her back to Ellis, she said, "Unbutton me."

Quickly he undid the buttons and she stepped out of the dress.

She was completely nude. Then she turned back to the peephole.

"No," Lee said. "Let's go see what they're doing in this room over here."

He took her by the hand and led her over to the next wall where there was another hole.

When he lifted the cover, she gasped.

"Oh my," she said.

"What are they doing?"

"There are two men and one woman. It looks like..."

Ellis moved her out of the way and took a look. "Yes, they're claiming her. One is taking her ass and one is taking her pussy." He stepped back. "That's what we'll soon be doing with you."

She moved back to the hole in the wall and watched. The woman seemed to be enjoying herself. One man was beneath her, and he was encouraging her. The other man was at her back and he was pushing into her ass.

"Oh," she cried "You're so big and full."

The man grinned at her. "Just the way you like it."

"Yes," she said and turned her attention to the man whose cock was entering her pussy. "You make it so tight."

The two men began to move in and out, each the opposite of the other.

The man taking her ass leaned back and popped her on the butt. "Squeeze me, Carmelito. Squeeze me tight."

"I am," she said. "You're just so big."

Mesmerized, Daisy stood there and watched as the two men ravaged the young woman's body. Her own body was beginning to heat and she felt Lee against her back, his head leaning in next to her.

"That will be you soon. Very soon," he said as he watched the people with her. "See how he's gripping her ass and bringing her back against him. He's pounding her with his cock. And I'm going to take your ass and do the same."

Her heart was beating rapidly in her chest, her breathing was fast and heavy and she knew she had to have her men now.

"Please, fuck me," she cried turning to face Lee. "I need you."

Ellis was beside her in a second and he picked her up and carried her to the bed.

They descended on her and she knew the first orgasm would be coming soon.

"Go watch the other rooms," Ellis told Lee. "I'll take care of Daisy."

They had come here to see if they could find Beth, but instead, now, Ellis was going to be taking care of her.

"Hurry," she said, gazing up at Ellis as he laid her onto the bed. He spread her legs and then quickly removed his clothes.

While he removed his pants, he stared down at her on the bed. "I'm going to punish you for making us bring you tonight. You had no business being here."

"How?" she asked. "By spanking my ass?"

"Yes," he said.

"How else?"

"Damn it, Daisy, you're testing me," he said, shucking his pants and then crawling up on the bed.

"First, I'm going to spank that naughty pussy of yours. Then I'm going to shove my cock so deep in your cunny that you're going to wish you'd stayed home."

His words did nothing but excite her more. She knew he would never hurt or harm her, but she did like pushing him. And she loved when he spanked her ass.

"Spank my pussy," she said with a moan. "I need to come."

"Not yet," he said, pinching her nipples. "Not until I say so."

This part she didn't enjoy. When he refused to let her come.

His fingers trailed down her body in a sensuous trail, causing her to jump when he found the butt plug.

"In just days, you will no longer need this thing and

instead it will be mine and Lee's cock plunging in and out of your tight little hole. Are you ready?"

A whimper came from her.

"Answer me," he demanded.

"Yes," she said, thinking how perverse it sounded, and yet, watching the man and woman through the peephole had eased so many of her worries. She could do this and experience both men at the same time.

"You and Lee claiming me, making me yours, that's what I want," she said with a gasp. "The two of you are what I need. Now."

He reached down and smacked her on the pussy and she jumped and moaned. "Ellis, please let me come."

"Not yet," he said.

This time, he lifted her buttocks and smacked her on the ass. She could feel her cheeks burning. Oh, how she needed him inside her.

"Ellis, please fuck me," she cried. "I need to come."

Lee walked over and began to remove his clothes. "Honey, my cock is near to bursting. You need to suck me."

When he was nude, he crawled onto the bed and placed his cock at her lips.

"Tell Ellis to let me come," she said.

He pushed her mouth onto his cock. "You need to concentrate on me coming. Ellis is in control of your pussy."

Eagerly she licked the bulbous head of his cock, her tongue swirling around the center. Unable to turn her head, she felt Ellis lift her hips, but before he placed his cock in her pussy, he pinched her clitty and she screamed around the cock in her mouth.

"Oh, darling, yes, just like that," Lee said.

Ellis began to shove his cock in and out and she clenched her pussy around his hard member.

She had a cock in her pussy and one in her mouth and she had yet to reach the fulfillment she so desperately needed after watching the two couples. Just the memory of the two men and one woman had her lifting her hips to meet Ellis's thrusts.

"Don't come, yet," Ellis told her once again. "I'm almost there."

"Me too," Lee said. "Just a little more. Oh, yes, darling like that. Suck on my dick."

She felt Ellis's fingers rubbing her little nub and she knew they were all close. It was all so incredibly wonderful that she didn't think she could hold back any longer. She lifted her hips and squeezed as hard as she could on Ellis's cock deep inside her, hoping this would push him along.

"Aargh," he cried his body tensing. "You may come."

Lee's cock surged in her mouth as he shoved it deeper and she felt her throat coated with his come.

"Yes," Ellis said, slamming into her again as her orgasm rippled through her, her body shaking as she came apart right there in a room in the bordello.

First, Lee pulled out of her mouth and collapsed beside her on the bed, then Ellis sank down on top of her. He pinched her nipple.

"Damn, woman," he said. "Maybe we should bring you to a bordello more often."

A grin spread across her face. "Do you think anyone is watching us?"

Her men both looked startled. "I don't know."

"Well, hopefully, we put on just as good a show as the ones we watched. The only thing that would have made it better is if you had both taken me."

Ellis smiled at her and Lee reached over and brushed a piece of hair away from her face. "Damn, Daisy. You surprise me more every day."

"In a good way?"

He laughed. "Yes. Most definitely in a good way."

Their hour was up and Daisy knew that Lee was concerned that he had not seen Beth. They slowly put their clothes on, and when everyone was dressed, they opened the door and walked down the stairs.

In the hour they had been upstairs, the place had become packed with men. The ladies were in demand. Her husbands placed her in between them as they walked through the crowd.

"Oh my God," she heard Lee say. "There she is. That's Beth."

Daisy glanced over and saw a young woman with an older gentleman, her face was pale and she did not look happy. But worst of all, her wrist was tied to his. She couldn't go anywhere.

CHAPTER 20

*R*age filled Lee as he rushed to Beth, knowing she was in trouble. Her eyes grew wide when she saw him coming and she shook her head, her mouth saying no.

"What the hell is going on here?" Lee said when he reached her side. "Who the hell are you?"

The man gave him a look that warned of retribution.

"George Richards. And you are?"

"I'm Beth's brother," he said. "What are you doing?"

Standing, the man was tall and broad and wore expensive clothing. "Your sister is my fiancé."

No, this couldn't be true. Beth would have written him and told him she was getting married.

"Is this true?" he asked, turning to look at Beth.

She licked her lips and he watched the man pull her tightly against him.

"Yes," she said, trembling.

"Do you love him?" Lee asked.

Tears welled in her eyes. "No, he's mean. He hurts me and now he's threatening to sell me to the madam. I hate him."

The man backhanded her and that was all it took. Lee jumped on him and started to pummel the man's face. He heard a whistle blowing in the background, but he didn't care. He had to save Beth. She was the last living member of his family and he couldn't let this man hurt her.

Ellis was next to him and he took his knife out and cut the ribbon between Beth and George while Lee punched him repeatedly in the face. Until suddenly he was being pulled off the man.

"What's going on here?" the sheriff asked.

"Arrest this man," George said, holding his bloodied nose. "He started a fight. All I was doing was entertaining this whore."

Beth gasped. "No, Sheriff, that's not what happened. He tied me up and dragged me in here. Told me that he was tired of me and he and the madam had a deal. When he got tired of a woman, he brought her here. He planned on selling me to the madam."

The sheriff's eyes narrowed and he shook his head. "You know, George, for a long time, I've turned my back on your nefarious ways because I didn't have any proof. But now I do."

The deputies surrounded George and they hauled him away. "You're going to regret this. I promise to run you out of town."

The lawman looked at Lee. "Why did you attack him?"

"Beth is my sister. I've been searching for her," he said.

Gazing at Lee, he looked between the two of them. "There is a family similarity. Take Beth and get out of town, now. Don't wait until the morning because George will be out and he'll gather his goons and they'll come after you. You've got maybe an hour. Already someone is going to be waking his lawyer to get him out of jail."

"What about the madam?" Beth said. "Is she going to get away with this?"

The sheriff smiled. "No, because she's getting shut down tonight. Now get out of here before all hell breaks loose."

Lee took Beth by the arm and Ellis grabbed Daisy.

"Thanks, Sheriff," Lee said and the four of them hurried out of the whorehouse.

Just as they were walking out the door, Lee heard the music stop and the sheriff raise his voice. "This here establishment is closed. Everyone, go home."

There was a loud rising of male voices.

"Hurry," Ellis said. "We need to get back to the hotel and get out of town."

The four of them hurried down the streets of Helena to their hotel.

An hour later, they were in the wagon with Lee riding shotgun beside Ellis, a rifle in his hand.

"How did you get involved with this man?" Lee asked in the darkness.

"He was nice to me. He took me out to dinner and

made me feel special. Sure I'd heard rumors but didn't believe any of them were true. Now, I can tell you everything I heard about him was true, but the worst was the way he would sell you to the madam. Thank you for coming to find me."

They rode along the trail in the darkness. Lee wasn't certain if the horses knew the way, but so far, the full moon was lighting their path and he wasn't about to stop.

"You'll stay with us in Treasure Falls."

"No, I can't," Beth said. "I'm getting on the next stage to a place called Blessing, Texas. I need to leave Montana and get away or George will try to find me. And if he does, he'll make me suffer."

As much as Lee didn't want to believe her, he feared what she said was true. She had to go away for a while. His heart seemed to shatter inside his chest. Why did it seem like all of his family had left him? First his father, then his mother, and now even Beth was leaving.

Once again, Lee was alone. Except for Ellis and Daisy. They were his family, and with them, he would create an even bigger family.

And if they had a daughter, he would kill the first man who tried to take advantage of her or who even looked at her wrong.

A coyote howled in the distance.

"Lee, I hate going off and leaving you, but it's for the best. In Texas, I'll be safe."

He sighed in the darkness. "I know. But that doesn't make it any easier."

Daisy reached back and laid her hand on the top of his that was gripping the side of the wagon. His chest jolted and he felt the connection with her all the way to his heart.

This woman was his destiny, his family. And together they would create their family.

CHAPTER 21

The next day before Beth left, Daisy managed to corner her. The woman needed to know how her own story had turned out. How sometimes leaving could be a good thing.

"Beth, can I speak to you for a moment?" Daisy asked.

They were going to the stage depot in less than an hour, and Daisy needed to tell her sister-in-law to remain strong.

"Your brother is a special man. And while I'm sure you don't understand our relationship, all I can say is that he and Ellis have been the best thing that's ever happened to me."

For the next ten minutes, she told her what Thomas Jones had done to her and how her father kicked her out into the streets. The girl's eyes widened and she grabbed her hand.

"I didn't really want to leave Charleston, but the new start was the best thing that ever happened to me. I'm happy and I hope that someday soon, you'll be happy as well."

The girl sniffed and then threw her arms around Daisy's neck.

"I'm so glad my brother has found someone he loves. I can see it in his eyes that he adores you. I'd like to find the same type of love."

Lee loved her? Daisy knew how she felt about her men but was waiting for a special time to convey her feelings. But for someone who knew Lee, to recognize the emotion, filled her with joy.

"Thank you," she said. "Now let's get you to the stage. Your brother is going to be devastated that you're leaving, but we all know it's for the best. But don't forget where we are. Write and if you ever have the chance, please come see us."

"You know I will," Beth said. "I just wish I could stay here and get to know you better. We're sisters now and I've always wanted a sister."

Daisy's heart beat quicker as she thought of her own sisters, how much she missed them. You never knew how important that connection was until you lost it.

"And you have one. Even though we're long distance." Daisy hugged the girl. "Be strong, Beth. You deserve happiness, just like I deserved happiness, and I think I've found mine."

An hour later, they put her on the stage, all of them crying as they said their good-byes. But Beth promised to write as soon as she arrived in Texas.

As they turned to leave, their hearts were heavy. And Daisy was filled with hate for men who took advantage of women. Why couldn't they let live and let live? Why did some men think women were easy targets who they could use to their advantage?

When they reached home, Lee glanced at her.

"Oh, there was a letter for you," Lee said, pulling out the envelope from his jacket.

"Me?" Daisy said then realized it could be from her sisters. She grabbed it and took it outside to read.

But it wasn't from her sisters. No, it was from her father. And his words stunned her.

Dearest Daisy,

I was wrong to take Thomas Jones's side. I should have believed my daughter and known she would never let a man do that to her.

For nights, I could not sleep for worrying about where you slept at night. Your mother has been angry with me ever since you left and then when we read the newspaper and saw where other women had come forward to say that Thomas Jones was a rapist, she's hardly spoken to me.

Believe me, I had no idea that such an outstanding citizen could be so despicable. He's been completely ostracized from society and is no longer the most eligible bachelor. In fact, no woman wants to be near him thanks to you and what you've done. Because I know my girl, I know you hung the sign on his gate.

It was a brilliant idea.

I'm begging for your forgiveness. I'm pleading with you to come home. You're my daughter and I was wrong not to realize the outstanding young woman you are. Please forgive me and come home to us.

Your loving father,

Papa

She reread the letter several times and tried in her heart to forgive him. He'd made a very costly mistake, and now it seemed he was paying for it. While it would do no good to harbor ill will toward her father, the most important thing she was proud of was that she had saved other women from Thomas Jones. Saved them from a predator but at a terrible cost.

Yet, just like she'd told Beth, she was so grateful for where she had landed. She had a beautiful home and two husbands who she had fallen in love with. A town that accepted her for who she was.

Yes, she was glad to receive the letter from her papa giving her forgiveness but that didn't seem to matter much anymore. What was important was right here in Treasure Falls. Her two husbands and hopefully soon, a family.

Standing, she walked inside the house. No, she would not be returning to Charleston. No, she would not be leaving her men. They were married and she was their wife. This was her home.

This was her destiny.

No longer was she desperate.

A sense of peace settled over her as she glanced around her home. Time to make supper for her men.

Taking the letter upstairs, she laid it on the dresser.

Then she walked into the kitchen and began to prepare tonight's dinner, a sense of rightness settled over her.

This was her life and she was glad. There was nothing for her back in Charleston. Nothing.

CHAPTER 22

*T*wo days later, Daisy walked down the street on her way home after taking lunch to her men. She liked to surprise them at the store. It gave her a chance to get out of the house and she enjoyed walking through the streets of Treasure Falls.

She felt safe here. After being here almost two months, Treasure Falls was beginning to feel like home.

Summer would be coming to an end soon and she knew that once they had children or even when winter arrived, she would not be spending a lot of time outdoors. Traipsing through the snow to the downtown area would not be smart.

The weather was wonderful in Montana. Warm with a slight breeze that cooled the evenings. Oh, how she missed the smell of the ocean, the seagulls, and even the ocean breezes, but this was now home. A home she was quickly growing to love.

While she was at the mercantile, she'd picked up a few

items she needed for their evening meal and as she walked along, she swung her basket back and forth and hummed a song.

It was a carefree summer day and she felt happy.

Her life in Treasure Falls was better than she could ever have expected, and though she missed her sisters, she could never see herself returning to the East Coast. Even now, she hoped and prayed she was expecting her first child.

Sometimes she thought she should send Thomas Jones a letter and thank him for destroying her life in Charleston, but quickly she would change her mind. The man deserved whatever happened to him.

Out of her ruination, she'd found a better life with two wonderful men she was falling in love with. She knew that soon they would both claim her and when they did, she would tell them they had given her a life she never expected and captured her heart in the process.

She loved Lee and Ellis more than her next breath. Nothing could or would ever come between them. She would die protecting her two big, burly husbands. Warmth filled her and she picked up her pace eager to get home and prepare their dinner.

As she walked through an alley shortcut, a man stepped along beside her, startling her. She could smell the liquor on him and she gave him her meanest look as he looked her up and down.

"So you're the whore those two married," he said with a growl.

A gasp escaped from her lips. She'd never seen this man before and she was shocked at his rudeness.

"Do not call me a whore," she said, stopping in the middle of the darkened alley, her voice rising. It was the middle of the day in the small residential area and no one appeared to be coming to her rescue. The urge to smack him was strong, but she resisted.

He grabbed her arm. "Look, girlie. Ellis Sanders killed my son and my daughter. Any woman who sleeps with that devil is a whore."

She was appalled he would dare touch her and confused by what he said about Ellis. She felt him pulling her and she punched him with her free hand.

"Get your hands off me," she cried. "Let go of me."

She pushed him, but the old man was stronger than he appeared. He began to drag her behind the buildings and her insides seized with fright.

"You're going to help me," he said. "Before I leave this earth, I'm taking Ellis with me."

Terror threatened to control Daisy and she struggled trying to get loose. "Don't worry, he'll kill you when he finds out you touched me."

The man laughed. "That would bring me peace. At least, then, I would be with my daughter and son and sweet wife. At least, then, I would not be alone."

Yanking on her arm, she almost fell. Then she reached out and kicked him on the shin.

"Bitch," he said and backhanded her.

For a moment, she was stunned as pain shot through her. Her face tingled and she knew that would probably get him killed, once Lee and Ellis learned he'd hit her.

"Now, come on, you're going to cook me one last meal before I die."

With her free hand, she rubbed her stinging face as she realized the man was serious. He was crazy if he thought she was going to cook for him.

"I'm not going to let you die," she said, wanting to deny him his last wish. "And you're not going to kill Ellis."

The old man rolled his eyes at her.

"I don't believe you when you say that Ellis killed your children. My husband would never harm someone. Not even you," she said. "This is a lie."

The old man spit on the ground.

"Who are you?"

"Henry Cox," he said. "My daughter was Arianna and my son's name was William. Don't ever forget their names."

Somewhere she remembered hearing those names. Was it from Ellis?

The birds chirped in the trees, and suddenly, she realized how she could leave clues.

As he pulled her onto a small side lane, she resisted. Slowly, she began to drop, one by the one, the items she'd purchased from the store on the path she knew her men took to walk home. Every few feet, she dropped an item until her basket was empty.

Afraid the basket would draw attention to what she was doing, she continued to carry the now-empty basket, certain her men would realize that something had happened. While they walked home, they would see her groceries lying in the street.

They were nearing a house and she kept glancing around, looking for anyone to help her. Henry had a death grip on her wrist and she knew she would be black and blue from his tight rein.

The cottage they neared was small and run down. And she so desperately wanted to find a way to keep from going in with him.

"I'm not going in there," she said.

He ignored her. "Today, I purchased a steak. I would like to have steak and mashed potatoes. I wish I'd bought the fixings for a pie, but I didn't think about it until just now."

The door hung haphazardly on its hinges. Paint was peeling off the outside of the house and it seemed to lean to the right.

"If you'll let me go, I'll fix you a pie," she promised.

Shaking his head, he turned his back on her.

"You're the bait to get Ellis here. But first I want one last supper. Then before I let him know you're here, I'll tie you up. When he walks in the door, he's a dead man," he said.

Rage filled her at the thought of him killing the man she loved. She took the basket and started to beat him about the head. "No, you're not going to kill Ellis. No. Help," she screamed.

"Stop it," he said. "Or I'll kill you right now. Do you understand me?"

He grabbed the basket and took it away from her, not noticing it was empty. The old fool didn't realize that she had left a trail almost to his door.

Turning the doorknob, he pushed her inside.

The stench of the place almost knocked her down. The house had not been cleaned in a long, long time and he expected her to cook in this house?

"You need a housekeeper," she said.

"You need to shut up and mind your own business," he replied.

"How can I cook when the stench of the place is enough to chase animals away," she said, glancing around at the clutter, the dirty dishes piled by a sink. "Do you even have clean dishes?"

"No," he said. "Probably not."

"Good grief," she said, walking inside farther. "I don't think Ellis killed your son or daughter, but your housekeeper..."

The man threw her basket at her and she ducked.

"You're being rude," he said.

Did he think she cared?

"If you're going to kill me or Ellis, what makes you think I'm going to be nice to you? You're not the first man who thought he could run over me and wouldn't you like to know what I did to him."

The man's eyes widened. For the first time, she could see a little fear reflected in his gaze.

"That's right, you should be afraid. Very afraid. You called me a whore and calling a decent woman that name just infuriates me. I might just poison you when I cook your last meal."

She watched the man's Adam's apple move up and down.

"My daughter took care of the house and she's been dead for many years."

Feeling the anger draining out of her, she glanced at the man as his shoulders seemed to sag.

"My son has been dead longer. He died in the mining accident," he said, going to his chair and sinking down.

"I'm sorry, but Ellis wasn't in town when the mine collapsed," she said.

"No, but he's still a Sanders. A damn Sanders," he said.

"You're not being fair. He lost his mother and father in that collapse. He lost just as much as you did."

The man's face turned red and he screamed at her. "Get in the fucking kitchen and make me a steak dinner. Do not come out until it's done. We're finished here."

Shaking her head, she couldn't resist. "You just want someone to blame, and Ellis is the convenient target. How did he kill Arianna?"

"She had a miscarriage," he screamed and dragged a whiskey bottle from the side of his chair and took a swig.

A miscarriage? Unless Ellis was the father, this could not be his fault.

"Go. Get in the kitchen, now, or I'm going to shoot you," he said and pulled a gun from the same place he'd found the whiskey.

She knew the gun was loaded because it appeared he kept it right next to him, and she wondered how many times he'd tried to kill himself with the weapon.

Could she sneak out after he became inebriated? Going into the kitchen, the first thing she saw were boards nailed across the kitchen door. No getting out without him hearing her.

She looked at the mess, the pile of dishes, the old food. A rat scurried away in the corner of the kitchen and she shivered. Maybe she should serve him the rat for dinner, but that would mean touching it. Another shiver went through her and she knew she could not touch the rodent.

With a sigh, she glanced out the window and hoped her men would see her trail of things she'd left behind. Hopefully, they would be here before she finished cooking his steak dinner.

How could a day that had been so wonderful, suddenly become so deadly? Looking around, she found a knife and an iron skillet. She'd let him drink a little more liquor and then she was going to take him on once again.

This time, the skillet would make a fine weapon.

After Charleston, she refused to be a victim any longer. By golly, she would take the man down herself if she had to.

CHAPTER 23

It was finally time to go home and Ellis couldn't wait. He'd been on edge all day after reading the letter Daisy's father had sent her. The man had admitted he'd been wrong and now he was begging his daughter to return home.

Would she?

"We need to talk," Ellis said to Lee as they walked home. Normally this was the time they unwound and often spoke about what was going on in the store and the bank.

"What's wrong?" Lee asked, turning and glancing at him.

"Remember that letter that Daisy received?"

"Yes," Lee said.

"She left it out and I read it," he said. "Our wife was innocent in the scandal that scalawag created and caused her to leave Charleston. Her father asked for her forgiveness and begged her to come home."

Lee sighed and shook his head as they passed along

the backside of a few buildings. "No. She's not going to leave us. I think she's happy. I know she makes me happy."

Their boots made crunching noises on the gravel in the alleyway. It wasn't far with this shortcut and it gave them some time to relax before they walked in the door.

"Agreed," Ellis said. "I'm happier than I have a right to be."

With his boot, Lee kicked a pebble out onto the street. "Someday I hope you realize that it wasn't your fault Arianna died. It was the will of God and no one else."

But Ellis should have been there for her. He should have been by her side. He should have been her husband. Instead, he'd let her father push him away.

"So our wife was innocent and now her papa wants her to come home," Lee said. "She could be expecting. No, she's not going to leave us. Why would a woman want to return to a place that treated her so badly? You're worrying about nothing."

"I hope like hell you're right," Ellis said, thinking he couldn't take another woman breaking his heart. Not again. And right now, Daisy had his heart all tied up. He hadn't planned on falling in love with her, but he would die protecting her and he couldn't watch her walk away from them.

Not after the joy they had found in each other's arms.

They walked along in silence, each man deep in his thoughts.

"Do you see that?" Lee asked.

"What?"

"There is a tin of flour lying back there. It looked like one that came from my mercantile. A brand new one."

"So," Ellis replied, "Maybe someone dropped it and will come back looking for it."

"There's a container of oats. Daisy bought oats earlier today."

Ellis jerked toward the container. They walked a little farther and there was another container and then some yarn.

"These are the items she purchased at the mercantile," Lee said. "Something is wrong."

They were almost to the house and they both began to run. Ellis was the first one through the door.

"Daisy," he yelled.

Silence.

"Daisy," he said, running up the stairs.

No one.

"She's left," he said, thinking he'd been right. "She's decided to return to Charleston."

Lee stood, shaking his head. "No. Somethings wrong. Check her closet. Are her clothes there?"

Ellis ran to the closet and the new dresses they had bought her hung in the closet.

"Then why is she not here? And why do I get the feeling those groceries have something to do with her disappearance?"

The two men stood staring at each other.

Suddenly it hit Ellis and almost knocked him to his knees.

"Henry Cox," he said. "Today is Arianna's birthday."

It must be the reason she was on his mind so much today.

"Those groceries are her letting us know where to find her," Lee said, running out of the room and down the stairs. "I'm going to kill that old man."

Ellis was right behind him. This time Henry had gone too far. In the past, Ellis had sympathy for him and he even felt some remorse, but not this time. This time Lee was right; he was going to kill him.

They ran out the door and began to follow the trail of their groceries, so glad that someone had not picked them up. The last one was twenty feet from Henry's door.

"Wait," Ellis said, grabbing Lee's arm. "Henry set this up. It's a trap for him to kill us."

"I don't give a damn," Lee said. "He's got Daisy."

They were both breathing hard from running the blocks to Henry's home.

"But if we go busting in there, then we give him what he wants. Let's look around a moment, check the windows and doors. Follow me."

How many times had Ellis helped Arianna sneak out of the house and escape her father? How many times had they met in the middle of the night? How many times had they gone to the pond where they spent the night together?

Right up until he'd asked her father for her hand.

They scurried around the side of the house and he peeked in the window.

"She's here," Ellis told Lee. Stunned, he watched his woman. "It looks like she's fixing him dinner."

"What? No, she wouldn't do that."

"There are potatoes boiling and a steak in a frying pan that she's searing."

Wondering what the hell was going on, he watched as she took a knife and a cast iron frying pan in her other hand and hid it behind her skirt.

"Oh, no. Our Daisy is about to get her revenge," he said. "Come on."

They ran back around the house to the front door and Ellis pulled out his Colt, kicked in the door, just in time to see Daisy raise the frying pan.

"Stop," he called.

Henry raised his gun and with a grin pointed it at Ellis. "I knew you'd come. You're a little earlier than planned. But I'll kill you and then eat my supper."

Ellis heard the gun cock and knew that he should feel a bullet enter his body at any moment, but he couldn't let Daisy kill Henry. As much as he hated the man for what he'd done, he was still Arianna's father. She'd loved him.

"You fire that gun, and I'm going to smack you with this frying pan," Daisy said. "I was just about to hit you when Ellis burst through the door and told me to stop."

The old man frowned. "No, I don't believe you. He would let me die."

"Henry, I loved Arianna. You're her father and I can't hurt you. If you want to shoot me, that's your choice, though I don't think Lee and Daisy are going to be happy."

Tears appeared in the old man's eyes. "She would have been twenty-five today. I would have grandchildren."

"I know," Ellis said. "I should have been there with her.

But your hate kept us apart. She wouldn't marry me because you told me no."

The man began to sob. "I didn't know she was pregnant."

"I didn't either," Ellis said, feeling the tears well in his eyes. "If I had known, we would have married against your wishes."

The man buried his face in his hands. "Why did you get her pregnant?"

"We loved each other very much," Ellis said, softly walking over to the man and taking his weapon. "When she refused to marry me, it just about killed me."

Daisy slowly lowered the frying pan and wiped tears from her eyes.

"I lost Arianna and then my son to that damn mine. There's no reason left to live. Shoot me and put me out of my misery, so I can go be with them."

Ellis didn't believe in superstitions. Or tales or anything else, but sometimes that didn't matter. Sometimes you just needed a little extra help. And today, maybe they needed to take a chance on a myth, he'd never believed in.

"I can't do that. But there is something we can do," Ellis said. "Maybe it would be good for both of us."

Lee walked around and pulled Daisy into his arms. "Are you all right?"

"I'm fine," she said. "Oh, I have to check on the steak."

"Wait here and I'll be back in just a few minutes," Ellis said, leaving Lee to protect their wife and keep an eye on Henry.

He ran back to the house and hitched a wagon and the

team of horses. When he returned to Henry's house, the old man looked dejected but ate his steak and potatoes.

Ellis tried to imagine how he must feel after losing everyone he loved but couldn't imagine. He glanced at Daisy fearful that she would be angry. He'd broken his promise of no more secrets between them.

As soon as Henry finished eating, they all loaded into the wagon. Lee and Daisy sat on the back bench while Henry sat next to him. Just before sundown, they pulled into the area that gave the town its name.

"Why are we here?" Henry asked.

"You know the legend?"

"No," Henry said. "All I know is that a lot of animals visit here at sundown."

Ellis told him the legend of Treasure Falls.

Henry stepped down from the wagon and walked to the pond. Lee helped Daisy out of the wagon and then they walked behind him.

Slowly Ellis approached the pond, his chest tightened when he thought of Arianna. She'd been his first love. And he would have happily married her, except she refused him once Henry told them no. But he hadn't known she was pregnant.

With a heavy heart, he moved next to Henry. "Henry, stop hating me. I loved your daughter with all my heart. I'm sorry about your son. It was a tragic accident. When you hate, you can never heal."

Suddenly a fish flounced and a ripple spread across the pond and then Arianna appeared as a reflection in the pond. Ellis stared in amazement.

Henry broke down and cried and reached his hands toward his loved one.

Arianna blew him a kiss before the reflection disappeared.

"Come back," he cried.

A shimmer appeared above the pond and the reflection shone bright like a nighttime star.

"Marianna," he said softly. "My love."

She held out her hand and Henry placed his palm in hers. She wrapped her arms around him, a glowing light shimmered about the couple.

There was a bright burst of radiance, and suddenly they both disappeared.

They all gasped.

"He's gone," Lee cried.

"What happened?" Daisy asked as they all peered into the pond.

The water was still.

"I think when she held out her hand, that was his signal it was time to go home to her," Ellis said, staring into the water.

Daisy walked over to Ellis and pulled him into her arms. "You, my husband, are an excellent man. I think you just helped your enemy. Arianna must have been a wonderful woman. Do you have any other secrets?"

"She was a wonderful woman," he said, thinking he was holding someone who he loved even more. "My only secret is that you're my love. My wife, my woman. She was the past and you are my future. And even that is a secret no more."

Daisy leaned back, her lips covering his. "Take me home, husband. I need both of my men."

Ellis took her hand and they walked to the wagon. He needed her as well. Tonight they would both claim their wife.

CHAPTER 24

$\mathcal{I}$t was dark by the time they arrived at the house. Ellis felt mentally exhausted. To think that Henry might have harmed Daisy frightened him. But he didn't think it would be a problem anymore.

"Go upstairs, undress, and wait for us," Lee told her.

From the tone of his voice, Ellis knew he was not happy. Daisy glanced at him, but then she hurried up the stairs.

"What's wrong?" Ellis asked, thinking what else could go wrong tonight.

"She was making him dinner," he said. "I think she needs to be punished. You don't make your enemies dinner."

Of course, the man was right, but Ellis thought she didn't have much choice. "Let's ask her why she was doing it before you decide to take her over your knee."

"That is a given. I'm feeling the need," Lee said.

"It might not be the night to show her your brute

strength," Ellis said, thinking he would much rather hold her in his arms and hope that the past was now completely behind them.

"We'll see," Lee said in a tone that wasn't his normal chipper self.

Ellis hurried up the stairs. Today, they could have lost her and that's what frightened him the most. If Henry had gotten his way, he could have killed all of them. Thank goodness, the man was just overly distraught. Grief had a way of doing that to a man. But that wasn't Daisy's fault.

When Ellis reached the top of the stairs, he hurried into their bedroom and began to remove his clothes. Daisy lay in position at the top of the bed, her face in the sheets, her ass sticking up in the air.

"Face us, we need to talk," Ellis said. He wanted to see her facial expressions to determine whether or not she had played any part in today.

"Tell us what happened this afternoon. How did you find yourself in Henry's house?"

The memory of not being able to find her when they looked in the house terrified him. While he liked that their wife had an empathetic nature, there were some people that were too dangerous to help.

"We were frightened he harmed you," Lee said, pulling his shirt from his pants. He sank down in the chair and began to remove his boots. Then he removed his pants, his big cock jutting out in front of him.

"Is that a bruise on your face," Ellis said, seeing the faint mark in the light from the lantern.

"Yes, he hit me when I fought him," she said.

Ellis glanced at Lee. She hadn't gone to Henry's home willingly.

For the next five minutes, she told them what happened and how she left a trail of groceries for them to find her.

Naked, he reached out and pulled her into his arms. "Thank God, you're all right. I knew you weren't there cooking him supper because you wanted to."

"No," she said with a sniff. "In some ways, I felt sorry for him, but since Charleston, I will fight and kick and scream whenever anyone tries to force me against my will. I'm never going to be a willing victim ever again."

Lee wrapped his arms around her. "I'm sorry for doubting you."

"You doubted me?"

"Yes," he said.

She reached up and stroked his face.

"In some ways, I did too," Ellis admitted. "I read your father's letter and I was afraid you had left to return to Charleston."

A gasp came from her and she sat back, her sapphire eyes flashed at them. "You are my husbands. My life, my world. I'm not going anywhere. I'm here to stay and I can't wait for us to create a family of our own."

She took a deep breath and then reached out and stroked each man's cheek. "These past weeks have been the best days of my life. You've shown me the meaning of love. I love you both with all my heart. You're my life, my family, my loves. Don't ever doubt me again."

Ellis chuckled. "Daisy, thank you for marrying us. You've healed my heart and made me into a better man. I love you, darling, and I now know better than to ever doubt you again."

She leaned in and kissed him gently before she released him and turned to Lee.

"Damn, Daisy, this is why I wanted to marry you. There's no guessing with you and I let my doubts get in the way. I gave you my heart on our wedding day. I love you, and I, too, will never doubt you again."

Pulling his head to her lips, she kissed Lee.

Standing, Lee walked over to the dresser where he selected a larger plug from the wooden box and a jar of ointment. "I want to see you work this plug into your ass. Afterward, I'm going to spank you and you are not allowed to come."

She tilted her blonde curls in one direction. "And why am I getting a spanking?"

"Because, darling, I was so damn scared tonight. No, it's probably not fair, but it will please me."

Her brows rose and then she smiled. "Just be fore-warned, that I will get you back. I'm going to make you scream with pleasure. I'm going to suck that big cock of yours until you're screaming my name."

Lee grinned.

Ellis stared down at his beautiful wife, her pussy beckoned him. The thought of plunging his long hard dick into her was tempting, but his pleasure would have to wait.

"Daisy, you enjoy us spanking you, and you have done well with us sticking a plug in your ass. Don't pretend you're not going to enjoy tonight."

Her eyes narrowed as she stared at him. "But you're not going to let me come."

The woman had a stubborn streak, and tonight she'd shown her spunky side when Ellis stopped her from hitting Henry with the frying pan. He'd been shocked, and yet he could understand why. She'd suffered enough at the hands of men who tried to ruin her.

She licked her lips and sighed. "What are you waiting for? I need my husbands, desperately."

Tonight was going to be a punishment for all of them, because right now, all he wanted was to slam her up against the wall and take her hard and demanding. But instead, he was trying to make certain she was ready for them both to fuck her, to take it nice and slow when he longed to plunge his cock into her.

"Put the butt plug in. Tonight, we're going to claim you, together. Lee will take your ass and I'll take your pussy."

Pursing her lips, she glanced between them and then took the plug. Lee handed her the lube and watched as she greased up the end. She placed the object between her legs but paused.

"Have I told you that I like the fact that you're in control? I like what we do together. I like it when you spank me, and I especially like it when you fuck me."

Lee groaned and she smiled at him in a tempting, saucy kind of way.

Ellis and Lee glanced at each other and Ellis knew they would not be too hard on her. Just hard enough to make her realize she had frightened them tonight, but they really just wanted to give her pleasure.

"Put it in," Ellis told her, placing a hand on her knee, she dropped her legs open wide. The sight of her wet, glistening pussy was almost more than he could bear. Her folds were shiny and slick, and the urge to climb onto the bed and sink into her was overwhelming.

Slowly, she inched the plug in, breathing deeply pushing and pulling, she bit her lip as the fake cock popped into place.

That was the largest and final plug. Tonight, they would finally claim her as theirs.

"Good girl," Lee said.

Glancing at him, Ellis could see sweat beads on Lee's lip and knew the man was in as much pain as he was watching their bride. They both wanted to fuck her.

Time for her punishment.

Reaching down, Lee swatted her ass to give her a taste of what was to come, hitting the plug. She gasped and turned her sapphire eyes on Ellis, dark and filled with lust.

"Over my knee," Lee demanded as he sank down onto the bed.

Ellis held out his hand and she placed her palm in his, curling her nails against his palm, scraping the inside. A shiver of need went straight to his groin.

After he helped her up, she lay over Lee's lap. The little witch looked back at Ellis and licked her lips, her tongue rolling across her full pink mouth.

Maybe she deserved this spanking after all.

Ellis's cock was throbbing, begging for attention, and he reached down to stroke it, rubbing the bead of come that spilled from the end.

Lee leaned down and kissed her on the ass, running his tongue along the seam of her cheeks, the plug peeking out.

"You're ours. No one messes with our woman. Do you understand?"

"Yes," she whispered.

Lee raised his hand and connected with her rounded cheeks. A handprint appeared on her white ass.

"Lee," she cried out, her hands searching for something to grip onto.

Smack, he hit her again and again in rapid succession.

A moan escaped her.

To change the rhythm, he spanked her first rapidly and then slowly and methodically, taking care to make certain her entire ass went from white to a blushing pink.

"Let me come."

For a moment, Lee paused and waited, hoping to keep her from coming.

Unable to resist, Ellis slid his fingers over her folds before plunging them inside her. Hot and moist, she was soaking.

"She's dripping."

"I'm not a water pump," she gasped, "to be talked about like I'm not here."

"Damn close," Ellis told her as he leaned down and put his fingers to her lips.

The woman was clawing at the nearby bed sheet, her long blonde hair splayed down to the floor, her breasts dangled like ripened fruit ready to be plucked.

Smack, Lee hit her ass again and again.

"Lee," she cried.

"Do not come. You do not have permission," Ellis warned.

"Please," she moaned.

She tried to rise, but Ellis put a hand on her back.

"All day, we couldn't wait to get home to you and you were gone. I was so afraid I'd lost you," Lee said.

Ellis pulled her up onto his lap and she wrapped her arms around his neck. "I'll never leave you."

Lee reached out his hand and stroked her hair. "We love you, Daisy. You're our wife, our bride, and soon the mother of our children. If something happened to you, it would be devastating."

Ellis rubbed her back. "Yes, we love you. Today showed us how much. With you, I want to create the family I never had. We've waited a long time for the perfect bride and it's you."

She raised her head and gazed at them. "I love both of you, and all I could think about was protecting you from Henry. Now please, fuck me."

Picking her up, Ellis laid her on the bed on her back. Immediately, she spread her legs, her pussy wet and glistening and so ready for them to take her.

A smile spread across her face. "Please, both of you take me. Make me yours."

"Yes," Ellis said with a moan, crawling beneath her and turning her to face him.

"I'm going to shove my cock in that sweet pussy of yours," he whispered against her mouth.

"Please," she groaned. "I'm yours. Take me."

CHAPTER 25

*S*taring into Ellis's eyes, she was both anxious and excited to see how it would feel being filled by both her men at the same time. Would it be as wonderful as when they took her virginity? Or would she hate it?

Already, her ass was hot, but beneath the pain was pleasure that rode her hard. Lying on the bed, nerves raced with anticipation and her body ached with need.

They loved her and she loved them and tonight was the culmination of that emotion and desire for one another. Never had she imagined that pleasure could come from pain. Never had she, a strong woman, thought that she would enjoy her men taking charge. Of them being rough and domineering.

But she trusted them enough to know that they would put her needs, wants, and desires first.

Never in a million years had she dreamed that two men would satisfy her in ways she never imagined. For weeks, they had stretched and trained her. Even now, the largest plug resided deep inside her, waiting for Lee to remove it.

Waiting for them to claim her ass.

Trembling, she knew she couldn't wait to feel them deep inside her at the same time. For their bodies and hers to be almost one. And hopefully a child would come from all the love right here in this bed.

Lee rubbed lube over his long, hard cock.

Ellis stared at her with his big emerald eyes. "Are you ready?"

"Yes," she whispered, wanting, needing them.

Tonight was the culmination of their love and these men she trusted with her life. They would take care of her and make her feel so very good.

Ellis lay back, his head on the pillows, his cock standing at attention. All for her. As she stared at his massive cock, her pussy clenched in anticipation.

Oh, how she wanted him deep inside her. Filling her, making her his.

"Ride me," Ellis said with a groan.

Gladly, she lifted her leg over him and climbed on top, her hands resting on his chest. Leaning on him, she realized the strength of Ellis.

Powerful and seductive. Her man.

The bed shifted and Lee climbed behind her. His tongue caressed her cheeks, sliding down, he licked her clit, before he sucked it into his mouth. A groan escaped from her lips, and she shoved back, needing more of his tongue, but he pushed her toward Ellis's cock.

"Oh, Ellis," she moaned. "Please put your cock in me."

"Is your pussy ready to grip me? When I bury my cock deep inside you, I'm going to go deep. I need to feel you squeezing me."

Unable to wait any longer, she rose above Lee and slid down over his hard cock, gripping his cock with her eager wet pussy. At the feel of him, she leaned back as she went lower and lower until she hit his pelvis.

The feel of his long, hard cock, snug in her pussy was almost enough to send her over the edge. The plug in her ass was tight against him.

All the pleasure from before returned like a wonderful storm battering her with greedy lust. Filled with cock and a plug, she was so full, so tight, and yet she wanted more.

She wanted Lee.

Once he was all in, she began to move up and down on Ellis's rigid member, rubbing her clit, needing to ride the pleasure building inside her.

Lee's hand caressed her buttocks, his hand rubbing her ass, pressing her back toward Ellis.

As she lay on top of Ellis's chest, her nipples brushed against his hair, rubbing and abrading them, he gripped her face and kissed her. A moan escaped her as their tongues tangled, and greedily, she needed more.

She wanted both of her men. She wanted to feel them deep inside her at the same time.

The feel of the plug being removed from her ass left her wide, empty, and bereft. Lee's fingers fondled her clit as a moan escaped her. But she needed more. She needed Lee.

Lee pressed the flared head of his hard cock against her trained ass and she moaned.

"Relax, darling," he whispered against her ear. "I'm going to make you feel so good."

And she knew he would, but still, the pressure of his invasion grew. Taking deep breaths, he slowly pushed his rock-hard cock into her, filling her. The tight ring of muscle gave way as his slick cock slid deep inside her.

"Oh," she cried as he slid in farther, then retreated, the feel of him hard and thick and so wonderful.

A hot rush of desire raced through her as she accepted him into her body, loving the feel of her men stuffing her. Pinned between them, she whimpered at how they controlled her completely. They began to move and she gasped, crying out at the rush of feelings.

They had promised her that she would love it when they claimed her and they were right. Heat coursed through her body and she could feel her orgasm rushing toward her.

First Lee, then Ellis, each one pushing her closer and closer to the edge as they retreated and filled her over and over. Between them, they brought her body to the brink of pleasure.

"Yes," she cried. "Please fuck me."

Ellis pounded into her with Lee retreating over and over. Between these two men was where she belonged. Here was her life. She needed the two of them to fuck her. To claim her. To make her theirs.

They were her men. Her husbands, her lovers.

"Let me come," she cried, knowing any moment she would go tumbling over the edge, falling into that blissful void.

"Never forget, you are ours," Lee gasped. "Yes, sweet-heart, you can come."

"Milk my cock. Take it deep and squeeze it," Ellis cried.

A bright burst of light overcame her as a scream tore through her throat and she squeezed and held her men, working the seed from their bodies. They were hers and she was theirs.

Nothing had ever compared to this moment.

Pleasure filled her and their hot seed coated her insides. Lee and then Ellis as they held her between them, their cocks buried deep inside her.

No barriers remained between them. They had marked her, made her theirs.

Breathing heavily, they slowly pulled free from her but held her between them. Nothing would ever be the same. Her life with her husbands was perfect in every sense of the word.

No longer was she a desperate woman living on the streets of Charleston. Now she was a queen, and her kings would always take care of her until the day she left this earth.

CHAPTER 26

Two years later, Lee gazed around at his beautiful wife while holding their son. The boy was a little tiger running around and getting into everything. But he loved him more than he'd ever thought possible.

Daisy sat on the couch breastfeeding their newborn daughter. She was barely a week old, and already, she'd captured their hearts. She had a head full of white hair and he thought she would be the spitting image of her mother.

Ellis was in the kitchen preparing dinner while Lee was on toddler duty. Lee had never been happier, and he hoped they had half a dozen more children.

Daisy glanced up at him and smiled. "I think she's asleep, but she hasn't turned loose of my nipple yet."

"Aw, I'm jealous," he said, smiling.

There was a knock at the door and Daisy, pulled up the blanket covering their daughter who lay sleeping at her breast.

Setting Lee Junior on his feet, the boy ran to the front

door. Lee followed behind him and slowly opened the door, grabbing the kid by the arm, to keep him from running outside.

Stunned, he stared in shock.

"Lee," his sister said with a smile.

A man stood behind her and she grinned. "I'd like to introduce you to my husband, John."

"Come in," Lee said, opening the door wider. Beth kneeled and gazed at Lee Junior who stood staring.

"Hi," she said. "I'd recognize that face anywhere."

His son wrapped his arms around his leg. "Come in and meet the baby. We have two children."

"And I'm expecting," she said with a smile.

"What brought you back?" he asked.

"John," she said. "He found me in Texas, and he told me it was time to come home to Montana. We fell in love but he left Montana and then when he returned, I was gone. I'm so glad he found me."

Instinctively, Lee reached out and hugged his sister, his heart filled with love. They were all back together and he was so glad.

"Beth, it's so great to see you."

"You, too, big brother. You too."

Just then, little Cora let out a squeal and it was the sweetest sound he'd ever heard. After wanting a family, his life was now full and Lee knew he was a lucky man.

Glancing at Daisy, she smiled at him and he realized she knew. She knew how much this moment meant to him. Thank goodness she'd come into their lives. Thank goodness she'd married him and Ellis.

And now he had everything he'd desired. A family of his own and his returning sister. Lee couldn't be happier.

* * *

DEAR READER, I hope you enjoyed this book as much as I did. Sometimes stories just flow from your fingertips and for me this one did. I loved Daisy and felt so bad for her. And Lee and Ellis become wonderful heroes. Yes, they will show up in other books in this series. Please be sure to leave a review of Our Desperate Bride. Reviews help authors and we like to know what you think of the book. Please leave a review.

Next up is Our Wild Bride. Can these cowboys tame this wild hellion of a woman. Let's hope so. For a sample of Blanche's story continue reading.

* * *

Our Wild Bride

BLANCHE UNDERWOOD GRABBED HER RIFLE, opened the window, and watched as the riders approached her home. Damn, damn, and double damn. It was that fella that her papa had lost the ranch to in a card game, and this time, it appeared he looked serious as he had brought the sheriff with him.

For months now, she'd resisted him.

Knowing it wasn't in her best interest, but unable to stop herself, she aimed the rifle and pulled the trigger. The bullet landed right in front of the new owner's horse and he had to fight to control the animal. Loud cursing filled the air.

"Serves you right for stealing my ranch," she said, pushing red hair out of her face.

It wasn't fair. This was her home, and her father had not only lost it in a card game, but then he had the audacity to die, leaving her alone. What was she going to do?

The sheriff continued toward the house. She knew better than to shoot at a lawman. Why had the new owner brought him out?

When the sheriff's horse reached the house, he stared up at her. She lowered her rifle and met him on the porch, wearing her pants and shirt. Skirts were beautiful, but they didn't fit the lifestyle of a rancher.

"Miss Underwood, that wasn't right."

"I'm just trying to keep vermin away from the ranch," she said, pulling her shoulders back and narrowing her eyes at the man, her trusty rifle by her side.

The man who claimed he owned the property rode up beside the sheriff.

"Sheriff, I've been a patient man," he said, glaring at Blanche. "But enough."

"It's not your property," she hissed.

The man held up the piece of paper that he claimed her father had signed.

"That's your father's X right there. Witnessed by Brent Harvey," he yelled.

"Brent Harvey is a liar and a cheat," she said, her voice

rising. "Anyone could've put that mark there. Even *you*." How many times was this man going to come out here and claim the land was his? She didn't believe him. It couldn't be true. And yet, she didn't have a good feeling about this little visit.

"Miss Underwood, you have no choice," the sheriff said. "Today is the twenty-seventh, and I expect you to be out of the house by the first. Mr. Jones will take possession then, and if that means I have to haul you out the door, then that's what I'm going to do."

Rage filled her, and she knew she was at the end of her rope. She'd run out of options, and while she could get a lawyer and take the man to court, she had no money. They all knew she was as poor as they came.

After all, she was but a woman trying to survive in a man's world.

And her big, beautiful house sat on one hundred acres of farmland perfect for cotton growing. Plus, a hundred head of cattle and twenty horses that were pure breeds.

Reaching for her rifle, she lifted it and aimed. "Get the hell off my ranch. It's still mine until the first. Get off now, both of you."

The sheriff shook his head. "Blanche, I know this is not the news you wanted to hear, but I have no choice. I suggest you pack a bag and get going."

But that was the problem. Where would she go? Her mother and father were dead, and she had no brothers or sisters. Her nearest relative was in Texas, and they didn't want her. She had no place to go and now she was losing her birthright.

With Papa's death and the loss of the ranch, she had nothing worth living for.

"Get out," she yelled. "I've still got three days. Get off my property, now."

She fired the gun into the air and the chickens squawked and ran from the yard.

The sheriff's face turned red. "I should arrest you. But I'm going to leave, but we'll be back on the first. Be gone."

This was it. This time the ranch would no longer be hers.

As soon as they rode away, the tears flowed down her cheeks. Sinking onto the steps, she laid her rifle down and began to cry. Great big hulking sobs.

What was she going to do?

Looking out at the pastures, she saw the cattle and the horses, and her heart cringed. She had three days. Half a week to sell everything she could. And then she didn't know what she would do.

Going into the house, she packed a suitcase of everything she wanted to keep. Glancing around the home, she knew there was so much she couldn't take with her. Grandma Rose's rocking chair. Her mother's spindle. Her father's...

Damn him.

It was so hard not to feel anger at what he'd done. For years, she'd tried to get him to quit gambling but he refused. Somehow that bastard Jones had tricked him; she just knew it.

She started to make piles of the things in the house. Items to sell, items to burn, items she couldn't live without.

It took her the rest of the day to get everything organized and part of the next day to get the animals ready.

Then she went into town and hung posters of the big sale out at the Underwood Estate. Everything must go.

As she was hanging a poster on a building, she saw another woman doing the same.

"Hello," she said, glancing at her. "What's this?"

"I'm a marriage matchmaker," the woman said. "I'm looking for girls to travel to Montana where there are eligible men looking for wives."

Blanche glanced at the poster again. "Good men?"

"Why, yes, and if you're not happy there, they will pay your way back to Charleston."

"Hrmph," Blanche said. What did she have here to return to?

"What kind of men are they?"

"Businessmen, ranchers, bankers, mine owners, all kinds of different men," the lady said, glancing at her. "Are you interested?"

Ranchers. There were ranch owners in Montana looking for a wife. She could live on a ranch, but in Montana, not the hellhole piece of plantation she owned in South Carolina.

Which was no longer hers.

No man around here was going to marry her. Her reputation as a wild woman was widespread, and yet, she hadn't really done anything. Only not been a woman who went to tea parties and acted all refined. A southern belle – oh no, not her.

No, she wore men's clothes, rode horses astride, cursed,

and shot a gun better than any man she knew. And if she wanted, she could out drink a man too.

But that would never get her married. If she went to Montana, she would need to learn to comport herself like a lady, whether she wanted to or not.

"If I signed up for this matchmaking in Montana, would you teach me how to be a proper lady?"

The woman smiled at her. "I'd do my best."

"When are you leaving? I'm not going to have a place to stay after tomorrow," she said, hoping that with the sale, she would have enough money to hold her over.

"I need three more girls and then we leave. But you're welcome to stay at my place until then," the lady said.

What should she do? Then it hit her. Mr. Jones may have won the ranch in a card game, but he only won the land.

Tomorrow night after she sold all the animals and the furnishings in the house, she'd have a big ol' cookout. She'd leave him with the land and that was it. As much as she hated Mr. Jones, he was going to hate her even more.

She was going to have a fire sale. Everything must go, including herself.

To continue reading buy at your favorite retailer!

PLEASE LEAVE A REVIEW

Did you enjoy the book? Reviews help authors. I would appreciate you posting a review.

Follow Lacey Davis on Facebook.

Sign up for my New Book Alert on my website and receive a free book.
www.AuthorLaceyDavis.com

Lillian Bradley sat astride a large red mare, gazing out at Texas's rolling hills, counting the cattle for a third time. Someone was stealing her cows.

With a sigh, her eyes roamed across the land she loved. All this acreage, cattle, goats, horses, and even a bunch of chickens, but they were all she had. Lily was alone.

Yellow fever had raced through her family, killing everyone but herself. Alone, she didn't understand how she had survived, but here she was with a large ranch and no one to help her with the many chores and responsibilities.

Some days, it was more than a body could bear, but she refused to give up.

Dust rose in the distance and she watched as a rider rode toward her. As the stranger drew closer, a groan rose in her throat. Jim White of the Big W Ranch, her neighbor, was coming for a visit. Rather an offer.

The man owned the largest spread in this section of Texas and was known for his shady deals, swindling, and even his prostitutes.

Pushing her long blonde curls back, her hand came to rest on the rifle she had become accustomed to being at her side.

He pulled his horse up beside her. "Good morning, Miss Bradley. How are you today?"

She turned and gave him an irritated frown. The wind blew her blonde hair into her face and she brushed it back. "Someone is stealing my cattle."

"I'm sorry to hear that," he said. "You know, a pretty young woman like yourself shouldn't be worrying over lost cattle."

"Maybe not, but yellow fever didn't give me much choice."

Her mare shimmied nervously, her paws dancing, eager to get away.

"Let me buy the ranch from you. Or even better, have you considered my son Matt? You are of marrying age. We could combine our land together into one big family ranch."

Like hell. She would shoot herself before she'd marry his weasel son.

"Thank you, but I'm not selling my family's land. Their deaths will not be in vain. As for marrying your son, no thank you."

It was all she could do to keep from screaming *oh hell no*. Not Matt White, a mean, cussing, tobacco spitting boy who knew his father would always get him out of trouble.

Mr. White's face turned red and his lips pressed into a thin line, but she didn't care. "A young woman should not be running a ranch."

"And yellow fever should not have killed my family." She sighed and turned to him. "For the last six months, I've taken care of this ranch and I plan on continuing. Need to find a new helper since Mr. Garza disappeared."

The man was like family and she was so disappointed he left her when she needed him the most. For nearly fifteen years, the man worked on the ranch and then one day, he just vanished.

"Miss Bradley," Jim said, his voice coaxing and gentle. "I could take the worry off your hands. You would be free to be the young woman you long to be."

It was true that she pined to have a carefree life again. One where all she had to worry about was helping her mother with dinner or the laundry. Where her grand-mother baked a cake every week. Her grandfather and she went fishing when the weather permitted. But those days were gone. Stolen from her by a hideous disease.

"I'm so glad you came by, Mr. White. If you know anything about who might be taking my cattle, tell them I'm a fine shot with a rifle and I will not hesitate to kill them. Also, if you see my helper, Mr. Garza, tell him I would like to talk with him about increasing his salary."

Often times, she worried something had happened to Mr. Garza. Because she didn't think he would have left without saying good-bye. At least, she hoped not.

"Will do, Miss Bradley. You think about my offer. I'm willing to give you top dollar for your ranch."

Top dollar, her ass. The man was a known cheat and would not give her anything for the Sweet B Ranch. Over the years, her father had complained how when times got bad, Ole Jim was there to steal the property for little or nothing from the ranchers in dire straits.

"Good day, Mr. White."

It was a clear signal for him to leave. She had an appointment with the banker later today and she needed to be riding into town but would wait until he was out of sight. Though she doubted he would do something, she could see him setting fire to the house to force her to sell.

The man was a vulture of the worst kind. Preying on the weak and, right now, she was in his sights.

What she needed was a husband. Someone to help her with the ranch. To keep rustlers from cutting the fence and stealing her herd. Someone to fill the house with love and laughter. Someone to help her create her own family.

The big house was empty and creaked and moaned at night. Fear had her sleeping on the horsehair couch her mother had been so proud of.

While she had managed on her own for six months, it was time for her to fill her bed. Someone to teach her the ways between a man and a woman. Someone to scratch this itch she knew only a man could fulfill. And she wanted someone to love her and the Sweet B.

Today, she'd donned her prettiest dress. This morning she bathed, fixed her hair with the hot iron, and made certain she looked her best.

She knew what she had to do. After she went to the bank, she planned on talking to the preacher about any eligible young men who might be interested in her as a wife.

It was time to go husband hunting. It was time to find herself a man.

To Continue Reading buy at your favorite retailer!

Also By Lacey Davis

Blessing, Texas Series
Loving My Cowboys
Two Cowboys' Christmas Bride
Two Cowboys One Bride
Two Cowboys Too Perfect
Two Cowboys to Protect Her
Two Cowboys Save Christmas

Bridgewater Brides World
Their Perfect Bride
Their Tempting Bride
Their Scandalous Bride

Treasure Falls Brides
Our Fugitive Bride
Our Desperate Bride
Our Wild Bride

Want to learn about my new releases before anyone else? Sign up for my New Book Alert on my website and receive a complimentary book. Blindfold Me. www.AuthorLaceyDavis.com

ABOUT THE AUTHOR

Lacey Davis is a pseudonym for a USA Today bestselling author who wanted to try her hand at writing sexy romance. With these novels, I hope to write sizzling romances that will leave you grabbing a fan to cool yourself off.

If you like hunky bad boy heroes who like to be in charge and strong pretty women who are willing to risk it all, then look no further. These sexy reads will get you in the mood. Come experience strong women who will tame these bad boys and leave them wanting more

The End

Printed in Dunstable, United Kingdom

71545759R00117